Jay Benson, fresh out of the U ...   ... vice –
three of them as a sniper in I...
His newly acquired ...   ... ith
much more to he...
The newly acqu...   ...n
– but quickly losi...
And the menacing ...   ... gang boss
with the propositio...   ...eo, up to killer
standards within nin...   ... ₱50,000 in it for you,
Benson.
Add a high-powered vic... ...ugs operation as only American
gangsterdom knows how to run one.
Have the whole hard-driving story structured by James Hadley
Chase – and you simply can't miss.

HADLEY CHASE IS *INSANELY READABLE*
The Observer

By the same author

JAMES HADLEY CHASE

Like a Hole in the Head

PANTHER
Granada Publishing

Panther Books
Granada Publishing Ltd
8 Grafton Street, London W1X 3LA

Published by Panther Books 1972
Reprinted 1974, 1975, 1976, 1977, 1979, 1980,
1984, 1985

First published in Great Britain by
Robert Hale Ltd 1970

ISBN 0-586-03781-0

Printed and bound in Great Britain by
Collins, Glasgow

Set in Linotype Plantin

Like a Hole in the Head

Chapter One

In theory it seemed to me to be a pretty bright, money making idea, but it only took around four months for the fact to sink in that The Jay Benson School of Shooting was headed for a flop.

Of course, I should have known. The previous owner, a nice old guy named Nick Lewis, had hinted that the school had long ago run out of powder. It was certainly ramshackle, and in need of a lot of paint. Against this it was plain to me that Lewis was long past good shooting and this, I told myself, was the reason why he had only six paying pupils, all as old and as doddery as himself. He had been running the school for twenty years. Over this period his books showed an impressive profit and it was only during the past five years the receipts had fallen off as his shooting had fallen off. I was confident enough to believe my shooting talent could put the school back on its feet, but I didn't take into consideration two important factors: my lack of working capital and the location of the school.

By the time I had bought the lease, the buildings and the three acres of sandy beach I had used up all my savings and most of my Army gratuity. Advertising in Paradise City and Miami comes high, and until I could make some kind of profit, advertising had to remain a pipe dream. Until I moved into the black, I couldn't afford to give the shooting range, the restaurant, the bar and our bungalow a much needed face lift. This, of course, turned into a vicious circle. Those few who were willing to pay to become good shots expected a decent restaurant and a comfortable bar. Those who did show up lost interest when they saw the set-up. They expected something in mink. They turned up their rich, spoilt noses when they saw the paint peeling from the buildings and that the bar carried only a bottle of whisky and a bottle of gin.

At least we had inherited Nick Lewis's six pupils, old, tiresome and hopeless as they were, but they did provide us with eating money.

Four months after we had opened, I decided to take stock. I looked at our bank balance ($1050) and our weekly turnover ($103) and then I looked at Lucy.

'We're not going to get anywhere unless we make this place fit for the rich and the idle,' I told her.

She fluttered her hands. This was a sure sign she was getting into a panic.

'Take it easy,' I said. 'Don't get excited. We can do quite a lot ourselves. Some paint, a couple of brushes, some hard work and we can put this place nearly right. What do you think?'

She nodded.

'If you say so, Jay.'

I regarded her. Every now and then, I wondered at the back of my mind, if I had made a mistake. I knew this school, if it was going to make money, had to be worked on. I couldn't do it alone. Maybe, if I had married a pioneer type of girl who could work as hard as I could, there would be less of a problem, but I hadn't wanted to marry a pioneer type of girl, I had wanted to marry Lucy.

Whenever I looked at Lucy, I got a lot of satisfaction. The moment I had seen her, I felt sure she was for me. We had run into each other in that strange way that destiny has for pairing off the male and the female.

I had just got out of the Army after serving ten years as a range instructor and three years in Vietnam as a sniper. I had ideas about my future, but no idea of getting married.

Lucy, twenty-four years of age, blonde, beautifully built, lovely to look at, was walking ahead of me along Florida Boulevard, Miami, where I had come for some sun while I made up my mind just how I was going to earn a living.

There are breast-men, leg-men, bottom-men and men who dig for the over-all female scene. I have to admit that a neat, small bottom that twitches as its owner walks has always caught my eye.

Lucy had the prettiest bottom I had seen and it so fascinated me that I followed it along the boulevard without being aware of the rest of her. As she passed a saloon a fat drunk came staggering out and cannoned into her. She went reeling across the sidewalk, heading helplessly towards the fast moving traffic. I was ten steps behind her. I reached her, caught hold of her arm and swung her against me.

She looked at me and I looked at her: those clear blue eyes, the snub nose, the freckles, the wide, scared mouth, the long silky blonde hair, the brave little breasts straining against the white cotton dress made a tremendous impact on me. I knew right away that she was the woman for me.

During my years in the Army I had met a lot of women. Experience had taught me how to handle the various types. I saw at once that Lucy was the timid, dithering type so I appealed to her kindness. I explained I was on my own, I had no friends and as I had undoubtedly saved her life would she have dinner with me?

She stared at me for a long moment while I tried to look lonely, then she nodded.

We saw each other every night for the next three weeks. I could see I had made an impact on her. She was the kind of girl who needed a man to lean on. At this time, she had a job as a book-keeper at a Pets' store on Biscayne Boulevard so she had only the evenings to herself. I took her by storm. I told her I had this chance to buy the shooting school and why I thought I could turn it into a paying proposition.

I had the reputation of being the second best shot in the U.S. Army. I had enough medals, trophies and cups to fill a small room. Also I had spent three years in the jungles of Vietnam as a sniper. I didn't tell Lucy I had been a sniper. I had a feeling I wouldn't get far with her if she knew that. Sniping is cold-blooded murder. It's a necessary job and I had got used to it, but it is something I never want to talk about. When I got my discharge, I had to look around for a new career. Shooting is my business. I have no other talents. When I saw the ad. that this school of shooting was in the market, I felt it was for me.

'Let's get married, Lucy,' I said to her. 'We can make a go of this school together. With your business training and my shooting, we can't miss . . . How about it?'

I saw the hesitation in her blue eyes. She was the kind of girl who dithered, not sure whether to go forward or to go back. I knew she loved me, but to her, marriage was a big step and she had to be pushed. I put pressure on her and turned on all my persuasive charm. Finally, after more dithering, she agreed.

So we got married and we bought the school. The first month was the sort of paradise I thought only came in dreams. I liked playing the boss-husband. Although she wasn't much of a cook and she would rather read historical romances than clean the bungalow, she was terrific in bed and she seemed to like being bossed around. Then, when the money didn't come in, when we had only these six old deadbeats paying us, between them, $103 a week and wasting my ammunition, I began to worry.

'It takes time . . . I must be patient,' I kept telling myself.

At the end of the fourth month, the position looked so bad, I decided Lucy had to accept some of the responsibility and I called this board meeting.

'We have to create a better image, honey,' I said. 'Then, somehow, we must advertise. The trouble is we are fifteen miles from Paradise City ... that's fifteen miles too far. If people don't know we are here, why should they come to us?'

She nodded.

'Yes.'

'So I'll buy some paint and we'll smarten the place up. What do you say?'

She smiled.

'Yes ... let's do it. It'll be fun.'

So on this bright late summer afternoon with a stiff breeze fanning the sand, the sea lapping the beach, the sun hot, the shadows growing long, we were both at work, slapping on paint.

I was working on the shooting gallery while Lucy worked on the bungalow. We had been at it since 05.00 with a break for coffee and another break for a ham sandwich. I was dipping my brush into the paint pot when I saw this black Cadillac come bumping up the dirt road that led to the gallery.

I put down the brush, hurriedly wiped my hands and stood up. I saw Lucy was going through the same motions. She too was looking hopefully at the big car as it came slowly up the drive, scattering sand and pebbles.

I could see two men in the back and the driver. All wore black, all had black slouch hats and they looked like three crows, sitting hunched up and motionless until the car pulled up within ten yards of the bungalow.

I started across the sand as a short, squat man got out of the car and paused to look around. The other passenger and the driver remained in the car.

Thinking back, I can see now that there was something menacing and vulture-like in the way this squat man stood, but that's thinking back. As I approached him, all I hoped for was this could be a profitable client. Why else, I asked myself, would he be here?

The squat man was looking at Lucy who was regarding him round-eyed, too shy to welcome him; then he looked towards me. His fat, swarthy face lit up with a smile that showed gold-capped teeth. He moved towards me, extending a small, fat hand.

'Mr. Benson?'

'That's me.' I shook hands. His skin was dry and felt like the back of a lizard. There was power in his fingers, but the grip was friendly without being challenging.

'Augusto Savanto.'

'Glad to meet you, Mr. Savanto.' Thinking back, this was the understatement of the year.

Augusto Savanto was around sixty years of age. I guessed he was Latin-American. His face was full and slightly pock-marked. He wore a straggly moustache that hid his top lip. He had flat, snake's eyes: genial, darting, suspicious and possibly cruel.

'I've heard about you, Mr. Benson. They tell me you are a fine shot.'

I glanced beyond him at the Caddy. The driver looked like a chimpanzee. He was small, very dark with a completely flat face, deep set tiny eyes and hairy strong hands that rested on the driving wheel. I looked at the man in the passenger's seat. He was young, slim, swarthy and he wore big sun goggles, a black tight suit and a startlingly white shirt. He sat motionless, staring straight ahead, not looking at me.

'Well, I guess I shoot,' I said. 'What can I do for you, Mr. Savanto?'

'You teach shooting?'

'That's what I'm here for.'

'Is it difficult to teach someone to shoot well?'

I had been asked this question before and I gave him the cautious, stock answer.

'It depends what you call well and it depends on the pupil.'

Savanto took off his hat to reveal thin, greasy hair and a bald spot on the crown of his head. He stared into the hat as if expecting to find something hidden in it, waved it in the air, then replaced it on his head.

'How well do you shoot, Mr. Benson?'

That was the kind of question I could live up to.

'Come over to the gallery. I'll show you.'

Savanto revealed more of his gold-capped teeth.

'I like that, Mr. Benson. No talk ... action.' He laid his small hand on my wrist. 'I am sure you are very good at hitting the bull, but can you hit a moving target? I am only interested in moving targets.'

'Would you like to see some clay pigeon shooting?'

He looked at me, his small black eyes quizzing.

'That's not what I call shooting, Mr. Benson. A burst with a shotgun ... what's that? One bullet from a gun ... that's shooting.'

He was right, of course. I waved to Lucy who put down her paint brush and came over.

'Mr. Savanto, meet my wife. Lucy, this is Mr. Savanto. He wants to see me shoot. Will you get some beer cans and my rifle?'

Lucy smiled at Savanto and offered her hand. He shook hands, smiling at her.

'I think Mr. Benson is a very lucky man, Mrs. Benson,' he said.

She blushed.

'Thank you.' I could see she loved this. 'I think he knows it. I'm lucky too.'

She ran off to collect some empty beer cans we keep for shooting practice. Savanto watched her go. So did I. Whenever Lucy took off, I was always looking after her. Her neat little bottom would never lose its charm for me.

'Beautiful woman, Mr. Benson,' Savanto said.

This was said very quietly and there was nothing but friendly admiration in the small eyes. I began to warm to this man.

'I guess so.'

'You are doing good business?' He was looking at the buildings and the peeling paint.

'We've only just started. A school like this has to be built up. The previous owner got old ... you know how it is.'

'Yes, Mr. Benson. This is what I call a luxury trade. I see you are painting the place.'

'Yes.'

Savanto took off his hat and looked inside it. This seemed to be a habit. After he had waved the hat around in the air, he put it on again. 'Do you think you can make money out of a place like this?' he asked.

'I wouldn't be here if I didn't.' I was relieved when Lucy came from the bungalow carrying my rifle and a string bag full of empty beer cans.

I took the rifle and she set off across the sand, carrying the string bag. We had often gone through this routine together and it was now close to a circus turn. When she was three hundred yards from me, she dropped the cans on the sand. I loaded the rifle, then waved to her. She began tossing the cans high into the air. She knew by now exactly the right height and just how fast to throw them. I hit each can. On the face of it, it was impressive shooting. When I had punctured ten cans, I lowered the rifle.

'Yes. Mr. Benson, you are a fine shot.' The little snake's eyes roved over my face. 'But can you teach?'

I rested the butt of the rifle on the hot sand. Lucy went off to collect the cans. We were no longer drinking beer: these cans still had a lot of work ahead of them.

'Shooting is a talent, Mr. Savanto. You either have it or you haven't,' I told him. 'I've been at it for fifteen years. Do you want to shoot the way I do?'

'Me? Oh, no. I am an old man. I want you to teach my son to shoot.' He waved towards the Cadillac. 'Hey . . . Timoteo!'

The swarthy man who had been sitting motionless in the back of the Cadillac stiffened. He looked towards Savanto, then opened the car door and came out into the hot sunshine.

He was built like a beanpole with big feet and hands: a shambling brittle-looking giant with hidden eyes behind the black sun goggles, a full mouth, a determined chin and a small pinched nose. He shambled across the sand and stood expectantly by the side of his father, dwarfing him by his lean height. He must have been around six foot seven. I'm tall, but I had to look up at him.

'This is my son,' Savanto said and I noticed there was no pride in his voice. 'This is Timoteo Savanto. Timoteo, this is Mr. Benson.'

I offered my hand. Timoteo's grip was hot, sweaty and limp.

'Glad to know you,' I said. What else could I say? He was a possible pupil.

Lucy had collected the beer cans and was now approaching.

'Timoteo, this is Mrs. Benson,' Savanto said.

The beanpole giant turned his head, then he took off his hat, revealing crisp black curls. He ducked his head, his face expressionless. The twin mirrors of his black glasses reflected the palms, the sky and the sea.

'Hello,' Lucy said and smiled at him.

There was a long moment of nothing, then Savanto said, 'Timoteo wants very badly to shoot well. Can you make him into a good shot, Mr. Benson?'

'I don't know right now, but I can tell you.' I offered the rifle to the beanpole. He hesitated, then took it. He held it like you might hold a puff-adder.

'Let's go over to the gallery. I can tell you when I've seen him shoot.'

Savanto, Timoteo and I walked across the sand towards the range. Lucy took the cans back to the bungalow.

Thirty minutes later, the three of us came out into the hot sunshine. Timoteo had fired off forty rounds of my expensive ammunition and had clipped the edge of the target once. The other shots had hummed out to sea.

'Okay, Timoteo,' Savanto said in a cold, flat voice, 'wait for me.'

Timoteo shambled away, reached the car, got in and settled down: a depressed-looking statue.

'Well, Mr. Benson?' Savanto said.

I hesitated. Here was a chance of making a little money, but I had to be honest.

'He hasn't any talent,' I said, 'but that doesn't mean he can't shoot straight if he's carefully coached. With ten lessons under his belt, you'll be surprised how he'll improve.'

'No talent, huh?'

'It might develop.' I was reluctant to kill a possible pupil. 'I can tell you after I've had him a couple of weeks.'

'In nine days, Mr. Benson, he must be as good a shot as you.'

For a moment I thought he was joking, then I realised he wasn't. The flat snake's eyes had become glittering bits of glass. His lower lip had turned into a thin line. He was serious all right.

'I'm sorry ... that's impossible,' I said.

'Nine days, Mr. Benson.'

I shook my head, controlling my impatience.

'It's taken me close on fifteen years to shoot well,' I told him, 'and I have talent. I guess I'm a pretty good teacher, but I just don't perform miracles.'

'Let us talk about it, Mr. Benson. It's hot out here. I'm not a young man.' Savanto waved his hand towards our bungalow. 'Let us get in the shade.'

'Why sure, but there's nothing to talk about. We'll just be wasting each other's time.'

He walked off slowly towards the bungalow. I hesitated, then followed him.

In nine days he must be as good a shot as you.

The boy would not only never make a good shot, but worse, he hated the feel of a gun. I could tell by the way he handled my rifle and by the way he flinched every time he pulled the trigger. He had held the rifle so loosely, his shoulder must be one black bruise right now from the recoil.

Seeing Savanto coming towards the bungalow, Lucy opened the front door, smiling at him. She had no idea what he had just said and she imagined I was about to sign up my first new pupil.

As I joined him, she said: 'Would you like a beer, Mr. Savanto? You must be thirsty.'

He regarded her, the genial smile back in place and he lifted

14

his hat. 'That is very kind of you, Mrs. Benson: not now; perhaps later.'

I stepped around him, opened the sitting-room door and waved him in. As he entered the room, I patted Lucy's arm.

'I won't be long, honey. You get on with the painting.'

She looked surprised, then nodded and went out into the sunshine. I moved into the room and shut the door, then crossed to the open window and looked out.

Lucy had gone around to the back of the bungalow. The black Cadillac stood in the hot sun. The driver was smoking. Timoteo was sitting motionless, his hands resting on his knees.

I turned around. Savanto had taken off his hat which he laid on the table. He lowered his bulk on to one of the upright chairs we had inherited from Nick Lewis. He looked around the room, slowly and with interest, then he looked at me.

'You don't have much money, Mr. Benson?'

I lit a cigarette, taking my time, then as I flicked out the match flame, I said, 'No . . . but why bring that up?'

'You have something I can use. I have something you can use,' he said. 'You have talent. I have money.'

I pulled up a chair and sat astride it.

'So?'

'It is vitally important that my son becomes an expert shot in nine days, Mr. Benson. For this I am prepared to pay you six thousand dollars. Half down and half when I am satisfied.'

Six thousand dollars!

Immediately, I thought what we could do with a sum like that.

Six thousand dollars!

We could not only give this place the complete face-lift it so badly needed, we could even run to a spot on the local T.V. station. We could hire a barman. We could be in business!

Then I remembered how Timoteo had handled the rifle. An expert shot? Not in five years!

'Thanks for your confidence, Mr. Savanto,' I said. 'I certainly could use money like that, but I must be honest with you. I don't think your son will ever be a good shot. Sure, I could train him to shoot straight, but that's all. He doesn't like guns. Unless you really like guns, you just can't be a good shot.'

Savanto rubbed the back of his neck and his eyes narrowed.

'I think perhaps I will have one of your cigarettes, Mr. Benson. My doctor doesn't like me to smoke, but sometimes the urge is too strong for me. A cigarette at the right time is soothing.'

I gave him a cigarette and lit it for him. He inhaled and let the smoke drift down his nostrils while he stared at the top of the table and while I thought of what Lucy and I could do with six thousand dollars.

Silence hung in the room along with our cigarette smoke. The ball was in his court so I waited.

'Mr. Benson, I appreciate that you are being honest with me,' he said finally, 'and this I like. I wouldn't be happy if you said you could make Timoteo into a good shot the moment I mentioned six thousand dollars. I know my son's limitations. However, he must become an expert shot in nine days. You told me you don't perform miracles. In a normal situation I would accept this, but this isn't a normal situation. The fact remains my son must become an expert shot in nine days.'

I stared at him.

'Why?'

'There are important reasons. They need not concern you.' His snake's eyes glittered. He paused to tap ash off his cigarette into the glass ash-tray on the table. 'You talk of miracles, but this is the age of miracles. Before coming here, I made inquiries about you. I wouldn't be here unless I was satisfied that you are the man I am looking for. Not only do you have a great shooting talent, but also you are very determined. During the years you served in Vietnam you spent long, dangerous and uncomfortable hours in the jungle, alone with your rifle. You killed eighty-two Vietcong ... cold blooded, brilliant shooting. A man who can do that is the man I am looking for ... a man who doesn't admit defeat.' He paused to stub out his cigarette, then went on, 'How much money do you want to make my son an expert shot, Mr. Benson?'

I moved uneasily.

'No amount of money can make him that in nine days. Maybe in six months, I might do something with him, but nine days ... no! Money doesn't come into it. I told you .. he hasn't any talent.'

He studied me.

'Of course money comes into it. I have learned over the years that money will buy anything ... providing there is enough of it. You are already thinking what you could do with six thousand dollars. With that amount of money you would be able to make a modest living out of this school. And yet six thousand dollars isn't a big enough sum to convince you that you can perform a miracle.' He took from the inside pocket of his jacket a long white envelope. 'I have here, Mr. Benson, two bearer bonds. I find them more convenient to carry around than a lot of cash. Each bond is worth twenty-five thousand dollars.' He tossed the envelope across the table. 'Look at them. Satisfy yourself that they are what I say they are.'

My hands were unsteady as I took the bonds from the envelope and examined them. I had never seen a bearer bond before so I had no idea if they were genuine or not, but they looked genuine.

'I am now offering you fifty thousand dollars to perform a miracle, Mr. Benson.'

I put the bonds down on the table. My hands had turned clammy and my heart was thumping.

'You can't be serious.' My voice was husky.

'I am, Mr. Benson. Make my son an expert shot in nine days and these bonds are yours.'

To gain a moment of time, I said, 'I don't know anything about bonds. These could be just pieces of paper.'

Savanto smiled.

'So you see, I am right when I said enough money buys anything. You now want to know if these bonds are forgeries. You no longer tell me that you can't perform a miracle.' He leaned forward, tapping the bonds with his finger nail. 'These are genuine, but don't take my word for it. Let us go to your bank and see what they have to say. Let us ask them if they will convert these two pieces of paper into fifty thousand dollars cash.'

I got up and moved to the window. The little room felt suffocatingly hot. I stared out of the window at the black Cadillac and at the beanpole sitting motionless in the back seat.

'That won't be necessary,' I said. 'Okay ... so they are genuine.'

Again he smiled at me.

'That is good for there is little time to waste. I will now return to the Imperial Hotel where I am staying.' He glanced at his watch. 'It is just after five o'clock. Please telephone me at seven o'clock this evening and tell me whether or not you will perform a miracle for fifty thousand dollars.'

He put the bonds in his pocket and stood up.

'Just a moment,' I said, annoyed with myself at sounding so breathless. 'I have to know why your son has to shoot so well and what his target will be. Unless I know, I can't hope to prepare him. You talk about an expert shot, but there are all kinds of experts. I must know, Mr. Savanto.'

He thought for a long moment. He had picked up his hat and was staring into it.

'So I will tell you. I made a foolish bet with an old friend of mine for a very large sum of money. My friend is an excellent shot and always boasting about what he can do with a rifle. Foolishly I said that anyone could become a good shot with training.' He regarded me sharply with his flat snake's eyes. 'Even I, Mr. Benson, when I have had too much to drink, can be stupid. My friend betted me that my son couldn't kill a fast-moving animal with a rifle after nine days' tuition. I was drunk and angry and I accepted the bet. Now, I must win.'

'What animal?' I asked.

'A monkey swinging in a tree: a deer in flight: a hare running from a dog ... I don't know ... something like that. My friend has the choice, but it must be a clean, certain kill.'

I wiped my sweating hands on the back of my jeans.

'How much did you bet, Mr. Savanto?'

He showed his gold-capped teeth in a smile.

'You are very curious, but I will tell you. I bet half a million dollars. Although I am a rich man, I can't afford to lose that amount of money.' His smile became fixed. 'Nor do I intend to.'

As I stood hesitating, he went on, 'And you can't afford to lose ten per cent of that kind of money either.' He stared at me for a long moment. 'Then at seven this evening, Mr. Benson.'

He left the room and started off across the hot sand towards the Cadillac. I watched him go. Halfway to the Cadillac, he paused, turned and raised his hat. He was saluting Lucy.

Fifty thousand dollars!

The thought of owning such a sum turned me hot with a frightening, terrible desire.

Fifty thousand dollars for a miracle! So I was going to perform a miracle!

*

I heard the front door open, then Lucy came in.

'Any luck, Jay? What was it all about?'

The sight of her brought me sharply down to earth. In those few moments as Savanto was driving away and Lucy was coming for news, my mind had been ablaze with the thoughts of becoming rich.

'Get me a beer, honey,' I said, 'and I'll tell you.'

'There's only one ... Shouldn't we keep it?'

'Get it!'

I didn't mean to speak so sharply, but I was pretty worked up and I wanted the beer because my mouth was dry and my throat constricted.

'Of course.'

She gave me a startled look and then ran off to the kitchen. I walked out of the bungalow and sat down on the sand under the shade of the palm trees.

Fifty thousand dollars! I kept thinking. God! It can't be possible! I scooped up a handful of dry sand and let it run through my fingers. Fifty thousand dollars!

Lucy came from the bungalow, carrying a glass of beer. She came to me, gave it to me and then sat down beside me.

I drank until the glass was empty, then I found a cigarette and lit it.

Lucy watched me.

'Your hands are shaking,' she said, her expression worried. 'What is it, Jay?'

I told her.

She didn't interrupt, but sat still, her hands clasping her knees, looking at me and listening.

'That's it,' I said, and we looked at each other.

'I just don't believe it, Jay.'

'He showed me the two bonds ... Each are worth twenty-five thousand dollars ... I can believe that!'

'Jay! Think a moment! No one would pay that sum of money without a good reason. I don't believe it.'

'I'd pay that sum of money to save half a million. Don't you call that a good reason?'

'You don't believe he made that bet, do you?'

I felt blood rising to my face.

'Why not! Rich men make big bets ... He said he was drunk at the time.'

'I don't believe it!'

'Don't keep saying that! I've seen the money!' I found I was shouting at her. 'You don't know anything about this! Don't keep saying you don't believe it!'

She flinched away from me.

'I'm sorry, Jay.'

I pulled myself together and gave her a wry grin.

'I'm sorry too. All that money! Think what we can do with it! Just think! We can turn this place into a dude ranch. We can have staff ... a swimming pool ... we can't miss! I've always thought with enough capital ...'

'Can you teach this man to shoot?'

I stared at her. Those words brought me down to earth. I got up and walked away from her, stopping a few yards from where she sat. She was right, of course. Could I teach this beanpole to shoot?

I knew I couldn't teach him to shoot for six thousand dollars, but for fifty thousand ... a miracle, I had said. This is the age of miracles, Savanto had said.

I looked at Lucy.

'This is a chance in a lifetime. I'll teach him to shoot if it's the last thing I do. Let me think about this. I have only an hour and a half before I telephone Savanto. If I say yes, I've got to know what I have to do. I've got to convince him and I've got to convince myself I can do it. Let me work it out.'

As I started across the sand to the shooting gallery, Lucy said, 'Jay ...'

I paused, frowning at her. My mind was already busy.

'What is it?'

'Are you sure we should get mixed up in this? I – I have a feeling ... I ...'

'This is something you have to leave to me,' I said. 'Never mind how you feel, honey ... this is a chance in a lifetime.'

I sat in the gallery and smoked cigarettes and thought. I sat there until it was close on 19.00 and by then I had convinced myself that I could earn Savanto's money. I had been one of the top range instructors in the Army, and God knows, I had had dozens of dopes through my hands who didn't know one end of the rifle from the other. Somehow, with patience, by shouting at them, by cursing them, by laughing with them, I had turned them into respectable riflemen, but a respectable rifleman is miles away from an expert shot. I knew that, but the thought of all that money lessened the problem.

I left the gallery and crossed the sand to the bungalow where Lucy was still painting the window frames. She looked at me, her eyes troubled.

'Have you decided?'

I nodded.

'I'm going ahead. I'll talk to him now. I'll need your help, honey. I'll go into the details after I've talked to him.'

I went into the bungalow. I looked up the number of the Imperial Hotel and after a delay, Savanto came on the line.

'This is Jay Benson,' I said. 'One thing I want to know before I commit myself. . . . Just how co-operative will your son be?'

'Co-operative?' I heard the surprised note in Savanto's voice. 'Of course he will be co-operative. He understands the situation. You will find him most willing to learn.'

'That's not what I mean. If I take him on, he's got to be more than willing. He's got to work at it, and I mean work. When do you have to put up?'

'September 27th.'

I thought for a moment. That would give me nine clear days, starting from tomorrow.

'Okay. From tomorrow at 06.00 until the evening of the 26th, he's mine . . . body and soul. He will stay here with me. He will do nothing but shoot, eat, sleep and shoot. He doesn't leave this range for a second. He will do everything I tell him to do and he won't argue, no matter what I tell him he is to do. I have a spare bedroom he can have. Until the evening of the 26th, he belongs to me . . . I'll repeat that . . . he belongs to me. Unless he agrees to these terms, it won't work.'

There was a pause on the line. I could hear Savanto's breathing. Then he said, 'It sounds as if you are thirsty for my money, Mr. Benson.'

'I am, but I intend to give you value for your money.'

'I think you will. All right . . . my son will be with you at 06.00 tomorrow.'

'How about my terms?'

'That is all right. I will explain everything to him. He knows how important it is.'

'I don't want any mistake, Mr. Savanto. When he comes here, he is mine. Is that understood?'

'I will tell him.'

'That's not good enough. I want your guarantee. He's mine or we forget it.'

Again there was a long pause, then he said, 'You have my guarantee.'

I drew in a long slow breath.

'Fine. Now I want some money. I'll have to buy a lot of ammunition. I must buy him a gun. He has to have a gun to fit him. He can't shoot with my rifle. His arms are too long.'

'You don't have to worry about that. I have bought him a gun: it is a Weston & Lees. I had it made for him. He will bring it with him.'

Weston & Lees were the top gunsmiths in New York. To buy

a made-to-measure gun from them costs around $5,000. He was right. If Weston & Lees had built a gun for his son I had nothing to worry about on that score.

'Okay. I want an advance payment of five hundred dollars,' I said.

'Do you, Mr. Benson? Why?'

'I am closing the school. I am getting rid of my pupils. I have bills to settle. We have to eat. I don't want anything on my mind except your son.'

'That is reasonable. Very well, Mr. Benson, you shall have five hundred dollars if it will make you happy.'

'That's the idea.'

'And you think you can make my son a good shot?'

'You said this is the age of miracles. I've thought about it. Now, I believe in miracles.'

'Good.' Again a long pause, then he said, 'I would like to have a final word with you, Mr. Benson. Have you a car?'

'Sure.'

'Then would you come to my hotel tonight . . . at ten o'clock?' He wheezed a little and then went on, 'I would like to finalise our arrangement. I will have the money for you.'

'I'll be there.'

'Thank you, Mr. Benson,' and he hung up.

Lucy was in the kitchen, cutting sandwiches. In our present state of economy, we had agreed that sandwiches were about the cheapest food we could live on. The previous day, I had bagged four pigeons and Lucy had spit-cooked them. With their breasts cut very fine plus a touch of Tabasco and a sliced pickle they made an acceptable sandwich.

I propped up the kitchen doorway.

'We have to have Mr. Savanto's son here, honey,' I said. 'For the next nine days, I've got to live with him eighteen hours a day. Is it okay to put him up in the spare bedroom?'

She finished cutting off the crusts of the bread, then she looked up. Those clear blue eyes were a little cloudy. Worry never helps anyone's face. For the first time since I had met and loved her she looked a little plain.

'Must we have him here, Jay? We've been so happy. This is our place.'

I remembered what my old man had once said. My old man had been a great talker and he had been very proud of his successful marriage.

Women are tricky, he had told me when I was too young to

care. My mother and he had had a little spat and I had listened, noting that my father had got the worst of it. When we were alone together, he had sounded off. I guess he was trying to justify his defeat. Maybe he was, but his words stuck.

'Women are tricky,' he said. 'You have to treat them with kid gloves if you want to get along with them, and there'll come a time when you will want to get along with one particular woman, so remember what I'm telling you. The right woman will be the pivot of your life: you'll find everything important revolves around her. A woman has different ideas from yours, but her ideas should be respected. But there comes a time when you know you are right, when you know you have to do this or that and she might not agree. You either do one of two things: you either spend a lot of time persuading her to see it your way or else you stamp over her. Either way works. The first way tells her you respect her opinion, but she is wrong: the second way tells her you're the boss ... and make no mistake about it, providing you are on the level, a woman wants her man to be the boss.'

I hadn't the time to persuade Lucy I was heading the way I had to head, so I stamped over her.

'Yes, he has to come here. We are about to earn fifty thousand dollars. Unless I have him here, we won't get the money. Nine days from now, we will be rich and we will have forgotten him. So he comes here.'

She hesitated for a brief moment. We looked at each other, then she nodded.

'All right, Jay.' She put the sandwiches on a plate. 'Let's eat. I'm hungry.'

We went out on to the patio.

I was disappointed that the thought of making all this money hadn't excited her as it excited me.

'What is it, honey? What's on your mind?'

We sat down in the sling chairs that creaked under our weight. Even when I knew she was worried I couldn't help thinking that before long we would get rid of these crummy chairs and have something lush on wheels with a sun umbrella clipped to its arm ... before long.

'The whole thing is crazy!' she burst out. 'You know it is! There's something wrong about it! All that money! That fat old man! You must know there's something wrong!'

'Okay, so it's crazy, but crazy things do happen. Why not to us? Here's a man rolling in money ... he makes a bet ... he ...'

'How do you know he's rolling in money?' she demanded, sitting forward and staring at me.

'For God's sake! I told you. He showed me those two bonds ... fifty thousand dollars. Of course he is rolling in money!'

'How do you know they aren't stolen ... forgeries?'

Kid gloves, my father had said. My gloves were beginning to wear thin.

'Honey. I've been offered a job of work ... something I can do. The pay off is more money than I've ever dreamed of. I will have to earn it. Okay. I wouldn't want so much money for nothing. This is a chance in a lifetime. He said I could go to my bank and check the bonds. Would a crook take such a risk?'

'Then why didn't you check them?'

'Will you let me handle this?' I was now using the tone of voice I used with the dopes who came to me to learn to shoot in the Army, but I was using more polite language. 'I'm doing what is best for you and for me. Let's skip the talk.... Let's eat.'

She looked at me, then away. We began to eat. I found I wasn't all that hungry. Lucy merely nibbled at her sandwich and finally, she dropped it back on her plate.

'You do realise we stand to make fifty thousand dollars, don't you?' I said when I could stand the silence no longer. 'You do realise what such a sum of money could mean to us?'

'I'd better get his bed ready. When is he coming?' She got to her feet. 'Have you finished?'

'Lucy! Cut it out! I'm telling you this is a chance in a lifetime! Fifty thousand dollars! Think! We're home! With that kind of money we won't have a care in the world!'

She collected the debris of the meal.

'It sounds wonderful ... not a care in the world.'

I let her go into the bungalow. I sat there in the growing darkness, staring at the moon as it crept out of the sea and continued its slow climb into the cloudless sky. For the first time since I had married Lucy, I was tense and angry.

I saw the light go up in the spare bedroom on the other side of the bungalow to our bedroom. Ordinarily, I would have helped her make up the bed. I liked to share the work around the place with her. I never liked to be far from her, but now, I let her make the bed. I just sat there, looking at the moon until it was time to get the car and drive into Paradise City.

I heaved myself out of the chair and found Lucy making coffee for tomorrow's breakfast.

'I have to go to the Imperial Hotel,' I said, standing in the doorway. 'Savanto wants to finalise this thing. I'll be back around eleven thirty. Okay?'

During the four months we had been married, I had never left her on her own on this lonely range. I knew she scared easily and I was annoyed with myself for not thinking of this when I had said I'd meet Savanto at his hotel.

But although her eyes were a little scared, she smiled.

'All right, Jay. I'll wait up for you.'

I grabbed hold of her and hugged her to me.

'Honey, this means everything to me,' I said and slid my hands down her slim back until I cupped her buttocks. I pulled her hard against me. 'I love you.'

'You scare me ... I've never seen you like this ... suddenly, you're so hard and tough ... you scare me.' She was speaking with her mouth against my neck and I could feel her trembling.

'Come on, Lucy,' I said, pushing her away. 'There's nothing about me to scare you.' I looked beyond her at the kitchen clock. It was close on 21.15. I would have to hurry. 'Lock up. Wait for me. I'll be back as soon as I can.'

I reached the Imperial Hotel a few minutes after 22.00. The hall porter told me Mr. Savanto was in the Silver Trout suite on the fourteenth floor. A snooty bus boy in a cream and scarlet uniform took me up, opened a door and waved me into a big, luxuriously furnished sitting-room. On the far wall was a big silver trout, lit by concealed lights and looking very opulent: a setpiece to please the customers.

Savanto was sitting on the balcony, overlooking the promenade, the beach and the sea, lit by the silver-white moon. As I walked into the sitting-room, he called to me and I joined him on the balcony.

'Thank you for coming, Mr. Benson,' he said. 'You had to leave your beautiful wife on her own. I should have thought of that. It was thoughtless of me.'

'She's durable,' I said. 'Have you talked to your son?'

'All business?' Savanto looked up at me and smiled. 'I am now satisfied that you won't fail me, Mr. Benson.'

'Have you talked to your son?'

He waved me to a chair.

'A whisky ... something?'

'No ... we're wasting time. What did he say?'

'He is a good boy. He does what I say. It is all right, Mr. Benson. Until the evening of the 26th he is yours, body and soul.' He paused and looked at me. 'That is what you want, isn't it?'

25

I sat down and lit a cigarette.

'What else do you want to say to me?'

'Looking at you now, Mr. Benson, I can understand how it was possible for you to have spent so many hours alone in the jungle, waiting to kill your enemies.'

'What else do you want to say to me?' I repeated.

He regarded me, then nodded with approval.

'Here is five hundred dollars.' He took from his wallet five one hundred dollar bills and offered them to me. I took them, checked them and then shoved them in my hip pocket.

'Thank you.'

'You tell me you are shutting the school and getting rid of your pupils?'

'That's right. They are a waste of money and time anyway. When your son arrives I will have no time for anyone else.'

'That is good. Has your wife any relations, Mr. Benson?'

I stiffened.

'What's that to do with you?'

'I was thinking it would be better for her to visit someone while you instruct my son.'

'If you mean she might take my mind off what I'm going to do, you're making a mistake. My wife stays with me.'

Savanto rubbed his jaw and stared for a long moment at the sea, glittering in the moonlight.

'Very well. Now there is another thing, Mr. Benson, you should know. It is absolutely necessary that no one ... I repeat that ... no one knows that you are instructing my son to shoot. No one ... especially the police.'

I felt a sudden prickle of apprehension crawl up my spine.

'What does that mean?'

'We are embarking on a deal that will make you wealthy, Mr. Benson. I am sure you are reasonable enough to expect certain rules which you, I and my son will respect. One of these rules is strict secrecy.'

'I heard you the first time. Why shouldn't the police know your son is getting instruction from me?'

'Because he would go to prison if it was found out.'

I tossed my cigarette butt over the balcony rail not caring if it landed on some dowager's wig.

'Keep talking,' I said. 'I want the whole photo.'

'Yes, Mr. Benson, I have no doubt that you do. My son is unfortunately tall. He is also very shy. He has many good points: he is kind, considerate ... he's well read ...'

'I don't give a goddam what your son is. Why shouldn't the cops know he is getting shooting instruction from me? What's this about prison?'

Savanto regarded me, his eyes glittering.

'My son went to Harvard. Because of his appearance and his shyness, he was picked on. From what I hear, he had a pretty bad time. In a moment of desperation he shot one of his tormentors who lost an eye. The Judge was understanding and wise. He realised that Timoteo had acted under the greatest provocation. There was a suspended sentence.' Savanto lifted his heavy shoulders. 'The Judge ruled that Timoteo must never touch a firearm as long as he lived. If he does, he must serve the suspended sentence of three years.'

I stared at him.

'And yet you made a bet that your son could become an expert shot in nine days?'

Again the heavy shoulders lifted.

'I was a little drunk. What is done, is done. I take it what I have told you doesn't alter our arrangement?'

'Not as far as I'm concerned,' I said after a moment's hesitation. 'If it leaks out he is using a gun that's your funeral ... not mine.'

'It could also be your funeral, Mr. Benson, because then you wouldn't get your money.'

'As I see it, my job is to teach your son to shoot,' I said. 'I don't want any complications. It's up to you to take care of the security. I'll be busy enough taking care of your son.'

Savanto nodded.

'I have already thought of that and I have made arrangements to take care of it. Two of my men will be arriving tomorrow with Timoteo. Neither you nor Mrs. Benson need bother about them. They will be there and not there, but they will look after security and they will also look after Timoteo if he gets difficult.'

I frowned at him.

'Is he likely to get difficult?'

'No ... but he is sensitive.' Savanto waved his fat hand vaguely. 'Nothing that can't be controlled.' He paused, then went on, 'You will impress on Mrs. Benson not to talk to anyone about this arrangement? You see, apart from the police, I wouldn't want my friend with whom I have made this unfortunate bet to know what is happening. I know he is curious. Security must be very strict.

'She won't say anything.'

'That is good.' He got abruptly to his feet. 'Well, then, tomorrow at 06.00.' He walked ahead of me into the brightly lit room with its lounging chairs in white and red satin, its cream-coloured carpet and the big silver trout on the wall. 'There is one other thing.' He crossed the room to a Chippendale desk, opened a drawer and took out an envelope. 'This is for you. It is a sign of trust and to give you encouragement, but you will have to earn it.'

I took the envelope, lifted the flap and looked at a piece of paper worth twenty-five thousand dollars.

*

As I drove up the sandy road leading to the shooting range, I spotted a red and blue Buick convertible parked outside the bungalow.

The sight of this car gave me a shock.

Who was visiting at this time of night? It was pushing 23.30. I thought of Lucy on her own, and my heart did a somersault. The excitement of having a bond worth twenty-five thousand dollars in my pocket vanished. I shoved my foot down on the gas pedal, roared up the rest of the road, slammed on the brakes and slid out of the car.

The light was on in the sitting-room, the windows were open and as I started for the front door, ready for anything, Lucy appeared before the open window and waved to me.

I drew in a breath and relaxed.

'Okay, honey?'

'Of course. Come in, Jay. We have a visitor.'

I opened the door and walked into the hall and entered the sitting-room.

A man in a light-weight well-worn suit was sitting in my favourite armchair. He had a glass of Coke in his hand and a cigarette dangled from his thin lips. I took him in with one quick glance. He was tall, wiry and tough-looking with a lined, sun-tanned face and clear, ice-blue eyes. His dark hair was cut close and his jaw line was aggressive. He got to his feet, putting the glass on the occasional table as Lucy said, 'This is Mr. Lepski. He wanted to see you. I asked him to wait.'

'Detective 2nd Grade Tom Lepski ... Police headquarters,' Lepski said and offered his hand.

Maybe for a split second I stiffened, but immediately I forced myself to relax. The ice-blue eyes were staring directly at me with that disconcerting stare all cops have. I was pretty sure he had noticed my reaction. Cops are trained to notice a thing like that.

'Trouble?' I asked, forcing a grin as I shook his hand.

Lepski shook his head.

'Sometimes I hate being a cop,' he said. 'Whenever I call on folk, they react like I'm going to make an arrest. It louses up my social life. Believe me, I'm a very sociable hombre ... like I was telling Mrs. Benson. No trouble, friend. I just missed you as you left. Mrs. Benson was on her own, we got talking, and hell! the time's rushed away. I guess my wife will be wondering where I've got to.'

'You wanted to see me?' I couldn't relax with this man. I was thinking what Savanto had said: *no one must know ... especially the police.*

'Jay, would you like a Coke?' Lucy asked. 'Do sit down, Mr. Lepski.'

'Sure ... I'll have a Coke,' I said. 'Sit down, Mr. Lepski.'

Lepski resumed his seat. Lucy went off to the kitchen and I sat on an upright chair, facing him.

'I won't keep you a few minutes, Mr. Benson,' he said. 'I shouldn't have come out here so late, but something is always cropping up and I was late getting away from headquarters.'

'That's okay. I'm glad you kept my wife company ... this is a lonely place.' I took out my pack of cigarettes, offered it and we lit up. 'I've been out on business.'

'Yeah ... Mrs. Benson was telling me.'

What else had she told him? I began to sweat.

Lucy came back with the Coke.

'Mr. Lepski wants you to sharpen up his shooting,' she said, handing me the Coke. 'I told him I didn't think you had time for a couple of weeks.' Seeing the way I was looking at her, she went on, 'I told him you had a special pupil you had to give all your time to.'

I drank some of the Coke. My mouth was as dry as sand.

'It's this way,' Lepski said. 'I've got my promotion exam coming up. I'm a pretty good shot, but it helps to get extra points. I wanted you to give me a few tips.'

I stared at the ice in my glass.

'I'd be glad to, but not just now. I'm sorry. As Lucy has told you I'm committed for the next two weeks. Can you wait that long?'

The ice-blue eyes began to probe my face again.

'You mean you've got someone to teach as important as that

29

'. . . who'll take up all your time for two weeks?'

'That's it. Can you wait? I would be glad to help you if you can wait.'

'It would be cutting it fine. My exam is at the end of the month.'

'I can give you two or three hours on 29th . . . any time convenient to you. That should be enough, shouldn't it?'

He rubbed the back of his neck. He was still looking thoughtfully at me.

'I guess so. How about 18.00 on 29th unless I call you?'

'Okay.' I stood up. 'I look forward to helping you.'

Lepski finished his Coke, then got to his feet.

'I see you're doing some painting around here.'

'Giving the place a face lift.'

'It sure needs it. Nick Lewis is an old friend of mine. He taught me to shoot. You know, I never thought he'd sell the place. Let's see, you've been here for four months? How's it working out?'

'Early days yet. We'll make out.'

'You should do. You've quite a reputation. Is it right you're the best shot in the Army?'

'Not now. I was rated the second best a year ago.'

'That's something! Those guys know how to shoot.' The ice-blue eyes probed again. 'I heard you were a sniper.'

'That's right.'

'Not a job I'd dig for, but I guess it calls for some pretty quick shooting.'

'It wasn't a job I liked either, but someone has to do it.'

'I guess that's right.' He started to move to the door, then paused. 'This pupil of yours must be a dope if you have to give up two solid weeks of your full time to teach him to shoot or does he want to be as good as you?'

'A rich man's whim. You know how it is. He has the money and he wants it exclusive. I'm not complaining,' I said as casually as I could.

'Anyone I would know?'

'No . . . he's here on vacation.'

Lepski nodded understandingly.

'Yeah . . . plenty of those here now. More money than brains and they don't know what to do with themselves.' He reached the front door, paused and shook hands. 'Unless I call you, I'll see you on the 29th.'

'That's it. Thanks for keeping my wife company.'

He grinned.

'It was my pleasure.'

Lucy joined me at the door and we watched him drive away. I took out my handkerchief and wiped off my sweating hands, then shut the door, locked it and followed Lucy into the sitting-room.

'I hope it was all right what I told him, Jay.' She was looking anxious. 'You look so tense. I thought the best thing was to tell him right away that you were tied up.'

'It's all right.' I sat on the table. 'It's just my bad luck he should have turned up.'

'Why bad luck?'

I hesitated, wondering whether to tell her what Savanto had told me. For a few brief moments I decided not to tell her, then I changed my mind. She would have to know. There was to be no more talk about Timoteo and she would have to be told why. So I told her.

She sat motionless, her hands between her knees, her eyes a little wide, listening.

'So you see this makes for complications,' I concluded. 'From now on, we mustn't say a word about Timoteo or his father or our arrangements to anyone. Understand?'

'Could the police involve you if they found out you were teaching a man who, by law, mustn't touch a gun?' she asked.

'Of course not. I'll say I didn't know.'

'But, Jay, you *do* know.'

'They couldn't prove it.'

'I also know. Do you expect me to lie to the police if they ask me?'

I pushed myself off the table and began to prowl around the room.

'I must earn this money. I'm hoping you will co-operate.'

'By co-operation, you mean I will have to lie to the police?'

I turned around, staring at her.

'Look at this.' I took the envelope from my pocket, took out the bond and laid it on the table. 'Look at this.'

She got up, walked to the table and bent over the bond. Her long, silky hair fell forward, hiding her face. She straightened, then looked at me.

'What about it?'

'That's one of the bonds I told you about. It's worth twenty-five thousand dollars. Savanto gave it to me. I can keep it, along with the other bond, when I have done the job. He means business, so we have to mean business . . . you and I . . . both of us.'

'Why did he give it to you when you haven't earned it?'

'To show he trusts me.'

'Are you sure?'

I was beginning to heat up again.

'Why else for God's sake?'

'It could be a psychological move.' She leaned forward, her eyes scared. 'You see, Jay, now you have this bond, you won't want to part with it. You'll be hooked with it.'

'So okay, he doesn't trust me, but he gives me twenty-five thousand dollars to get me hooked. He doesn't have to do that! I'm hooked already! I know what money this big can do for us! I'm going to earn it! I'll teach that guy to shoot if I have to kill him!'

She stared at me as if she were looking at a stranger. Then she moved to the door.

'It's getting late. Let's go to bed.'

'Just a minute.' I found a pen, wrote my name and address and my bank account number on the envelope, put the bond in an envelope and sealed down the flap. 'Will you go to the bank first thing tomorrow, Lucy, and tell them to hold this for me? I would do it myself, but Timoteo is coming at six and I have to make a start with him. Will you do that? Will you also get in a stock of food?' I took two of the hundred dollar bills Savanto had given me from my wallet. 'Buy enough food for a week and get in a lot of beer.'

She took the money.

'All right.'

She went along the passage to the bedroom. I knew for the first time since we had married, she was unhappy. The thought nagged me. I stood looking at the envelope. I had to think of our future. She would snap out of it in time, I told myself. I had Timoteo on my mind. For the moment, she had to take second place.

Carrying the envelope, I went into the bedroom. She was in the bathroom, taking a shower. I put the envelope under my pillow, then sat on the bed, waiting for her.

Neither of us slept much that night.

Chapter Two

We got up at 04.45, and while Lucy heated the coffee, I took a shower and had a shave. Although I had slept badly, I was now more relaxed. I had a job of work ahead of me, and when I'm working, I'm always in a good frame of mind. During the past four months when I had had so little to do except worry about our finances, I had been getting slack and irritable. That doesn't mean I hadn't enjoyed having a lazy time with Lucy, but enough was enough. I was ready to go to work again.

I found Lucy sitting on the patio, sipping her coffee and watching the sun come up behind the palm trees.

'When Timoteo arrives,' I said, taking the cup of coffee that was waiting for me on the table, 'you won't see me until lunch time.' I sat down by her. She looked a little wan and still worried, but this wasn't the time to worry about her worries. I would have to shelve that problem until later. 'I want you down at the bank by nine o'clock. When you get back, will you telephone our six pupils and tell them we are closed until the end of the month? I don't think they'll care. Colonel Forsythe might be tricky. Turn the charm on. Tell him we just have to paint the place. I am sure you can handle him.'

'All right, Jay.'

'Get enough food in to last a week.' I hesitated, then went on. 'Watch your cooking. His father is paying the bills. He'll expect to be well fed. We have five hundred dollars to cover the expenses.'

Panic showed in her eyes.

'All right, Jay.'

I smiled at her.

'Now don't flap. We are about to earn fifty thousand dollars. Remember you are as important as I am in this deal. I'm relying on you to take everything off my back except teaching this guy to shoot.' I finished my coffee and lit a cigarette. The first cigarette of the morning is always my favourite. 'Everything good that comes to me, I want to share with you.'

She pressed her hands together.

'Is it this job or the money that has made you change?' she asked in a low voice.

'Change? I haven't changed. I don't get it.'

'You have changed, Jay.' She looked up and forced a smile. 'When you told me the first time we met that you had been an army instructor, I found it hard to believe. You weren't like an army man ... you were so kind, so understanding to me. I couldn't believe you could handle men, give orders, be ruthless. It puzzled me.' She paused. 'I see now why you will teach this man to shoot. I'm a little scared of you now. I do see you have to be rough and hard if you are to succeed, but please try not to be tough and hard with me.'

I got up and pulled her out of her chair and took her face in my hands.

'No matter what, Lucy, remember this: I love you. I am the luckiest guy alive to have found you. Go along with me for a few days, then it will change. You'll look back on this and you'll forgive me if I've hurt you and you'll see what I'm doing now is right for both of us.'

We were kissing, holding each other and I was even forgetting what was ahead of me when the sound of an approaching car parted us.

'Here they come,' I said. 'Okay, honey, I'll see you at lunch time.'

I moved off the verandah into the sun.

Coming up the drive was a small truck. Two men were in the front seats. The driver, seeing me, waved his hand, then steered the truck towards me.

I waited.

The truck pulled up and both men got out. The driver was middle height, wearing only a pair of black boxing trunks. His body was covered with thick, coarse hair. He was around thirty years of age with a fleshy, swarthy face. If you like the Dago type – I don't – you could call him handsome. He was certainly sexy and in fine condition. Flat muscles rippled under his skin. He could be as quick as a lizard and as strong as a bull.

My eyes shifted to his companion. He was older, shorter and he wore one of those Hawaiian shirts that have dropped out of favour: yellow flowers on a red background and a pair of grubby white slacks. His swarthy face was pock-marked, his eyes small, his lips thin and his nose broad and flat. He looked like one of those types you see on TV, playing a minor moronic gangster.

The driver came towards me, revealing perfect white teeth in a wide, know-all smile.

'Mr. Benson? I'm Raimundo. I'm Mr. Savanto's right hand, left hand and possibly left leg.' His grin widened. 'This is Nick. Don't bother about him. No one does. He's just the jerk who sweeps up the horse droppings.'

As he didn't offer his hand, it saved me from shaking hands with him. I didn't like him. I didn't like his companion.

'What are you doing here?' I asked.

'We've got things for you, Mr. Benson.' He suddenly looked beyond me and his eyebrows went up. I glanced over my shoulder. Lucy was moving into the bungalow, carrying our cups. She was wearing a halter and cotton jeans. As she moved, her bottom gave a little twitch.

'Is that Mrs. Benson?' Raimundo asked, his eyes moving back to me.

'That's Mrs. Benson.' I gave him the hard eye. 'What things have you brought?'

'The works: the rifle, ammunition, food, booze. I haven't missed a trick.'

'What do you mean ... food? We're capable of buying our own food.'

His grin became sly. 'You don't have to ... it's all here with Mr. Savanto's compliments.'

He turned to his companion who was standing indifferently by the truck.

'Hey, Nick, get the stuff unloaded.' He turned to me. 'Is that the shooting range over there? We'll unload the ammunition there if it's okay with you.'

I hesitated, then shrugged. If Savanto wanted it this way, he was the boss and it would save me money.

'Where's Timoteo?'

'He's on his way. He'll be here any minute. Have you somewhere we can pitch a tent? Me and Nick won't bother you. We have our own food. Nick knows how to take care of me.' Again the wide grin. 'Just say where we can be out of your way and that's where we'll be.'

'What are you going to do around here?'

'Security. We'll wander around out of sight. If anyone comes here, we'll ease him off. No rough stuff, Mr. Benson. All done with charm. That's what Mr. Savanto said and what Mr. Savanto says goes.'

I pointed to some distant palm trees: over five hundred yards from the bungalow.

'Anywhere beyond those trees.'

'Okay. I'll give Nick a hand.'

He strolled over to the truck. I returned to the bungalow. I had an itchy feeling down my spine: the feeling I used to get in the jungle when I was sure one of the Vietcong was moving in my direction. Lucy had come out on to the balcony and was watching.

'Who are they?' she asked when I reached her.

'Two of Savanto's men. They have brought provisions.'

She stared at me.

'Provisions?'

'That's it. Savanto is providing the food so that saves you a shop-up.' I looked at my watch. 'Show them where to put the stuff, honey.'

She looked helplessly at me, hesitated, then moved down the steps towards the truck. Both Raimundo and Nick were coming towards her, staggering under the weight of two wooden cases.

Raimundo gave her his sexy smile.

'Plenty of good food here, Mrs. Benson,' he said. 'Where do you want it put?'

At this moment I saw the black Cadillac coming up the drive.

'Here he is, honey. I'll leave you to handle this,' and I started across the sand to meet the car as it pulled up.

The driver who looked like a chimpanzee slid out of the car, opened the rear door, then ran around to the boot, opened it and took out a suitcase.

Timoteo Savanto got slowly out of the car and stood awkwardly in the sun as I approached him.

He was wearing a black short-sleeved cotton shirt, black cotton slacks and black rope-soled shoes. He looked like a stork that had fallen in tar.

'Hi, there,' I said and offered my hand.

He ducked his head: his face was anonymous with his eyes hidden behind the black goggles. He took my hand in his limp, sweaty clasp and immediately released it.

'Come and see your room,' I said. 'Would you like a cup of coffee?'

'No, thank you. No ... I've had all I want.' He looked helplessly around.

'I'll show you your room, then let's get over to the range.'

'It doesn't matter about the room. I'm sure it's all right.'

'Fine ... it is.' I turned to the Chimpanzee. 'Take the bag to the bungalow. Mrs. Benson will show you where to leave it.'

Raimundo and Nick were coming out of the bungalow, having got rid of the two cases.

Raimundo lounged up to me.

'Nice little place you have here, Mr. Benson,' he said chattily.

'The stuff's all delivered.' His eyes took in Timoteo and his smile became an insulting jeer. 'Hi, Mr. Savanto: you all ready for the bang-bang act?'

I saw Timoteo cringe and turn red.

I've had to handle lots of smart boys during my time in the Army. I decided to crack down on this hairy know-all right away.

'Get the ammunition and the rifle to the range!' I barked at him, using my Army voice that can carry a quarter of a mile. 'What the hell are you hanging around here for?'

If I had hit him across the face he couldn't have looked more startled, but only for a moment, then he stiffened. His face turned viciously hard and his eyes glittered with fury as he glared at me.

'You speaking to me?'

Every now and then I had run into the tough guy who didn't react to a barking voice. Then I had to throw my rank at him, but I had no rank to throw at Raimundo. That didn't worry me. I had Savanto's twenty-five thousand dollar bond behind me and I was sure, strong as he was, in a knock down and drag out, I could take him.

'You heard me, glamour-boy! Get the stuff delivered and quit flapping with your mouth!'

We looked at each other. For a moment I thought he was coming at me, but somehow he managed to control himself. He forced a vicious grin.

'Okay, Mr. Benson.'

'And wipe that goddam grin off your face,' I snarled. 'I don't like it.'

He looked quickly at Timoteo, then he looked beyond me at Nick who was gaping at me.

'You don't have to talk this way to me,' he said.

I spotted the uncertainty in his voice. He wasn't scared of me, but he was scared of his boss.

This was the time to dig in the blade and turn it.

'Don't I?' My parade-ground voice bounced off the roof of the bungalow. 'Who the hell are you? I talk anyway I like! I'm the boss around here! If you don't like it, get the hell out of here and tell your boss! Tell him what you told me: you're his right hand, his left hand and possibly his left leg. He might just laugh himself sick but it's my guess he won't. Get this stuff delivered and then get lost!'

There was a long explosive pause. Raimundo had turned

grey under his tan. He seemed unable to make up his mind whether to go for me or surrender.

'No one . . .' he began, his voice quivering with fury.

I had him on the run and I knew it.

'Hear me!' I bawled. 'Get lost!'

He hesitated, then walked slowly to the truck. He climbed into the driver's seat and started the engine. Out of the corner of my eye I saw Nick climb in beside him. The truck moved off and headed for the range.

I looked at Timoteo who was standing, transfixed. The black sun goggles were pointing my way. I assumed he was looking at me, but I couldn't swear to it.

I grinned at him.

'I don't like that guy,' I said. I purposely softened my voice. 'I'm an ex-Army man. When I don't like a guy, I bawl him out. Are you sure you wouldn't like a cup of coffee?'

He gulped, then shook his head.

The driver of the Cadillac who had been watching this little scene, came over.

'Excuse me, sir,' he said to me. His flat Chimp face was tight and his breath whistled through his flat nostrils. 'Okay for me to speak to Mr. Savanto?'

At least I had put the fear of God in him.

'Go ahead,' I said and walked over to the bungalow where Lucy was standing under the roof of the verandah. I knew she had seen and heard what had happened. I wanted to reassure her.

She looked at me as I reached her, her eyes very wide and shocked.

'I had to handle him, honey,' I said quietly. 'He's a trouble maker. Just relax. Now he's been told, he'll stay told.'

'Oh, Jay!'

I saw she was shaking.

'Come on, baby, snap out of it.' I gave her a quick kiss. 'Don't let my Army voice scare you.' I grinned at her, trying to be reassuring, but she was staring at me, bewildered and still shocked. 'It's a trick. You just bawl and you get things done. Come on, honey, I've got things to do.'

'I'm sorry, Jay.' She made an effort to pull herself together. 'I've never heard a voice like that. I couldn't believe it was coming from you.'

'Like I said, it's a trick . . . it's Army.' Again I grinned, but it was a little forced. I knew I was wasting valuable time. 'You'll go to the bank?'

'Yes.'

'If there's anything else you want, buy it. Have you looked at the food they've delivered?'

'Not yet.'

'Well, look at it. If there's anything missing, get it. Okay?'

'Yes.'

I heard the Cadillac start up. Turning, I saw the car heading down the drive. Timoteo Savanto still stood where I had left him in the sun. He had his hands clasped behind his back and he was looking after the departing car. Even with the sun goggles hiding his eyes, he looked like a pet dog watching his master leave him.

'I have to take care of Timoteo,' I said. 'See you lunch time.'

I left her and walked across the sand. When I came up to Timoteo he stiffened and turned his goggles towards me.

'Let's go over to the range and have a talk.'

Beyond him, I saw the truck moving away from the shooting gallery and head towards the distant palm trees.

We walked in silence to the gallery and entered the cool, dim lean-to. Away from us were the targets, a hundred yards out in the hot sunshine.

By one of the wooden benches were two cases of ammunition and a rifle in a canvas case.

'This your gun?'

He nodded.

'Sit down and relax.'

He lowered himself on to the bench as if he expected it to collapse under him. His thin swarthy face was covered with sweat beads. His hands shook and jerked. He was as fit for a morning's target practice as an old lady who finds a burglar under her bed.

I've had them before: the guys who hate guns, who hate the noise a gun makes, who can't see anything exciting in using a gun well. There are two ways of handling them in the Army. First, the sympathetic approach, gentling them along as you gentle a nervous horse. Then if that doesn't work, you scare the crap right out of them, and if that doesn't work, you forget them, but I knew I couldn't forget Timoteo. He wasn't a man: he was a fifty thousand dollar bond.

'I've an idea you and I will get along together,' I said. I sat on the other bench and took out my packet of cigarettes. I offered it.

'I – I don't smoke.'

'That's fine. That helps. I shouldn't smoke, but I do.' I lit a cigarette and drew smoke right down into my lungs, then breathed out slowly. 'As I said, you and I will get along: we have to.' I grinned. 'You have a tough job ahead of you, but I want you to know I'm here to help you. I can help you, and I'm going to help you.'

He sat there and stared towards me. I couldn't tell his reaction. The goggles hid the expression in his eyes, and men's eyes are important to me when I'm sounding off.

'Can I call you Tim?'

His eyebrows came together, then he nodded.

'If you want to.'

'You call me Jay ... right?'

He nodded.

'Well, Tim, suppose I take a look at the gun your Dad has bought for you?'

He didn't say anything. He shifted on the bench and looked helplessly towards the gun in its canvas case.

I stripped off the case and examined the gun. As I knew it would be, it was a beautiful job. Weston & Lees don't produce anything but beautiful jobs. If he couldn't shoot with this gun, he wouldn't shoot with any gun.

'Very nice.' I broke open one of the boxes of ammunition and loaded the gun. 'I want you to look at the first target on the left.'

He turned his head slowly and stared across the hundred yards of sand at the target.

'Just keep watching it.'

The gun wasn't built for me, but in the Army I had to use a lot of guns that weren't built for me nor for anyone else. I braced myself. To me, it was easy shooting. I fired off six rounds. The centre of the target came away and fluttered to the sand.

'You're going to shoot like that pretty soon, Tim. Hard to believe, isn't it? I assure you you will do it.'

The black goggles gaped at me. I could see myself in their twin reflections. I saw I was looking tense.

'Will you do me a favour?' I asked, forcing myself to relax.

There was a long pause, then he said in husky voice, 'A favour? I've been told to do anything you say.'

'You don't have to do *anything* I say, Tim, but will you take those sun glasses off?'

He stiffened and reared back, his hands going protectively to the goggles that were forming a wall between us.

'I'll tell you why,' I went on. 'You can't shoot behind sun glasses. Your eyes are as important as your gun. Take them off,

Tim. I want your eyes to get used to the light here which is pretty strong.'

Slowly, his right hand reached for the goggles like a virgin taking her pants off in mixed company. He hesitated, then slowly the goggles came off.

Now I saw him for the first time. He was younger than I thought: maybe around twenty, not more than twenty-two. His eyes altered the whole of his face. They were good eyes: direct, honest and without guile: the eyes of a thinker, but right now they were also frightened eyes. He was no more like his father than I was like Santa Claus.

*

I was sitting by Timoteo's side, explaining the parts of the rifle to him when Lucy appeared in the doorway.

I knew I was wasting time going over the rifle with him, but I wanted him to relax, to get to know me and to stop shaking. This was the gentling process. I spoke quietly. I was trying to will into him that this rifle could come alive in his hands, could obey him, could be his friend. I didn't say all this crap in so many words, but I tried to convey it. So far, my words were bouncing off him like a golf ball against a concrete wall. But years as an instructor had taught me that often just when you were despairing, you get the break-through. Lucy's sudden appearance broke the beginning of his concentration and sent a rush of blood to my head.

'I'm sorry, Jay,' she said, seeing the way I reacted. 'I didn't mean to disturb you...'

'What is it?' The snap in my voice made Timoteo stiffen. It also made Lucy take a step back.

'The car won't start.'

I drew in a deep breath. I looked at my watch. I was surprised to see I had been talking to this beanpole for close on an hour. I shot him a quick look. He was staring down at his feet and I could see a vein in his forehead pounding. Lucy and my barking voice had undone the work of an hour.

I put down the rifle.

'What's the matter then?'

She looked like a kid caught with her fingers in the jam.

'I – I don't know. It just won't start.'

I made an effort to hold down a burst of temper and succeeded, but only just.

'Okay, I'll come.' I put down the rifle. Then to Timoteo, I said, 'I won't be a moment. Stay here now your eyes are getting used to this light. Don't put those sun glasses on.'

He mumbled something, but I was already moving to the door. Lucy fell back, giving me room to pass.

'Did you put your foot hard down on the gas pedal?' I asked as she trotted alongside me to keep up with my strides.

'Yes.'

'A hell of a time for it to play up. Well, I'll get it going.' I was sure she had done something stupid and it infuriated me that she had come to me just when I was getting this goddam beanpole in a more relaxed state of mind.

The Volkswagen was parked under a palm thatched lean-to. I jerked open the door, slid into the driving seat, sure that under my hand, the car would start.

Lucy stood by watching.

I jiggled the gear lever to check it was in neutral, then I shoved the gas pedal to the floor and switched on. I got a noise, but no start. I did this three times. Finally, the noise convinced me that the engine wasn't going to fire. I cursed under my breath, my hands resting on the steering wheel as I glared through the dusty windscreen. I weighed up the importance of making the car start against the importance of getting Timoteo to shoot.

I had this twenty-five thousand dollar bond. This was like having twenty-five thousand dollars in cash. This bond had to be lodged in the safe keeping of a bank. Suppose someone stole it? Suppose our bungalow caught fire and the bond got destroyed? I was now responsible for it. I could imagine Savanto's reaction if I had to tell him I had lost it.

I got out of the car, went around to the back and opened the lid. I looked at the engine. When a car makes the noise this one is making, the first thing to do, if you know anything about cars, is to check the distributor head and be prepared to clean the points. So I looked. The distributor head was missing.

That cooled me. My temper and my irritation with Lucy went away. Again I felt that itchy prickle run up my spine.

'No wonder you couldn't start it ... the distributor head has been taken away. Have you the bond with you?'

With wide eyes, Lucy stared at me, then opened her bag and gave me the bond.

'I never expected it would be easy, honey,' I said. 'No one can earn money this big without sweating for it. Now listen: there was something Savanto said to me which I haven't told you. He said you would be best off away from here while I'm teaching Timoteo to shoot. I can call a taxi and you can go to a hotel. We have the money, and it will be only for nine days. What do you say?'

'I'm not going!' Although she looked scared, she also looked determined.

'Fine.' I put the bond in my hip pocket, then went to her, and put my arms around her. 'I don't want you to go. Go and keep Timoteo company while I talk to Raimundo. It's my bet he's taken the distributor head.'

'Be careful, Jay. That man frightens me.'

'He doesn't frighten me.' I kissed her, then set off across the sand towards the distant palms.

It was a longish walk in the sun and I was sweating by the time I was within sight of the truck.

Raimundo and Nick were pitching a tent. They had picked a good spot. There was shade, plenty of beach and the sea. As I approached, I saw Nick, his Hawaiian shirt black with sweat, doing most of the work. Raimundo was singing. He had a good voice. It sounded good enough to come out of a transistor.

He stopped singing when he saw me, turned and said something to Nick who looked up, stared at me and then went on driving in a tent peg.

Raimundo came towards me. He moved well, and he was very sure of himself.

I stopped when I was within six feet of him. He stopped too.

'You have the distributor head of my car,' I said. There was a bite in my voice, but I wasn't bawling. 'I want it.'

'That's right, Mr. Benson. I have it ... orders.'

'I want it,' I repeated.

'Yeah.' His grin widened. 'Mr. Savanto gives orders too: he said no one comes in; no one goes out. That's his idea of security. You call Mr. Savanto if you don't believe me.' He cocked his head on one side. 'You're doing your job. I'm doing mine. The truck doesn't work either.'

I thought fast. Savanto could have given this order. We had no reason to leave the range now except to put the bond in the bank. If Savanto considered security so important, he wouldn't want either Lucy or myself to leave the place, and yet this could be Raimundo's way of getting even with me for the way I had bawled him out.

'I'll talk to your boss,' I said. 'If you're being smart, I'll be back and you'll be sorry.'

'You do that.' He was very sure of himself. 'You talk to your boss. He'll tell you.' He threw a lot of weight on the word *your*. It wasn't lost on me.

I walked back to the bungalow. It was a long walk. I didn't hurry. It was now getting too hot to hurry and I had some thinking to do. If what Raimundo had said was true, then I had a problem on my hands. I had in my hair twenty-five thousand dollars that didn't belong to me.

I reached the bungalow and walked into the sitting-room. I went over to the telephone and lifted the receiver. There was no dialling tone. The telephone was as dead as an amputated leg.

I sat down in my favourite armchair and lit a cigarette. I sat there for some minutes thinking. No car ... no telephone ... fifteen miles from the highway. To say we were cut off was an understatement.

I wasn't fazed. This kind of situation was something I thrive on. I got to my feet, went into the kitchen and inspected the food that had been delivered. It was quite a selection: at least we wouldn't starve. I went over the dozens of cans of food: all of the best and enough to keep three adults eating well for a couple of months. There was an impressive selection of drink including six bottles of champagne, lots of canned beer, whisky, gin and tomato juice.

So being cut off from Paradise City wasn't a problem. But what was I going to do with this bond which didn't belong to me?

I thought about the problem, knowing I was wasting time, but this was important; more than important.

Finally, I went to our store cupboard and found a small empty biscuit box. I put the envelope containing the bond into the box. Then I found a roll of adhesive tape and taped the lid to the box.

I left the bungalow by the rear door and crossed over to a row of palm trees that gave the bungalow its only shade. I paused to look around the way I had so often looked around before setting up an ambush in Vietnam. When I was satisfied I was on my own and no one was watching me, I scooped a deep hole in the soft sand under the third palm tree in a row of five and buried the biscuit box against the tree root. I smoothed down the sand. It took me some minutes to get rid of my footprints around the tree. I was finally satisfied.

I dusted the sand off my hands and looked at my watch. The time was 09.26. Timoteo had been on the range for close on three and a half hours and he hadn't fired a shot.

I hurried across the sand towards the shooting gallery. I felt under sudden pressure. If I was going to teach this beanpole, I just could not have any further trouble. And even before I made a start to teach him, I had to get him relaxed!

I reached the gallery. The sand deadened my footfalls. I heard Lucy's voice. She sounded animated. I slowed, then stopped in the shadow of the lean-to and I listened.

'I was like you before I met Jay,' she was saying. 'You may not believe it but I was. I'm pretty bad now, but I am better. Before I met Jay I was so mixed up, just looking in a mirror made me jump. I guess it was my father . . .' A long pause, then she went on, 'They say most kids when they are in a mess blame their parents. What do you think?'

I rubbed the sweat off my face and edged closer. This was something I wanted to hear.

'It's as good an excuse as any.' I scarcely recognised Timoteo's voice. He too sounded animated. 'We are all looking for excuses. Maybe our parents are to blame, but we're to blame too. It is a comfort to us to say if our parents had only been different. There are special cases of course, but I think we just have to help ourselves.'

'You're lucky to be able to think like that,' Lucy said. 'I know my father was a lot to blame.'

'For what?'

'For why I am a mess. You see, he wanted a boy. He was set on it. When he got me, he just refused to accept me as a girl and I couldn't have been more girl. He always made me wear trousers. He always expected me to do the things boys do. Finally, he realised it was hopeless, then he dropped me . . . ignored me. All the time I was struggling to get some love from him. To me love is important.' A long pause, then she asked, 'Don't you think so?'

'I wouldn't know.' Timoteo's voice was suddenly flat. 'I've been brought up in a different way. Didn't your mother give you love?'

'She died when I was born. How about your mother?'

'Women don't count in the Brotherhood. I scarcely ever saw her.'

'Brotherhood? What's that?'

'A way of life . . . something we don't talk about.' Again there was a long pause, then he said, 'You said you're in a mess. Why do you say that? I don't think so.'

'I'm in less of a mess than I was, but I'm still messy. I have no confidence in myself. I feel inadequate. I scare easily. I almost die if there's a thunderstorm. I was much worse before I met Jay. You mustn't think because he shouts and scowls he isn't kind and understanding. He is ... anyway, you'll find out. I don't know why I'm talking like this.' She laughed. 'You looked so depressed and worried, the same way I know I look sometimes, I just couldn't help sounding off.'

'I appreciate it, Mrs. Benson.'

'Please call me Lucy. After all you're going to live with us. I know we're going to be friends.' A pause, then she asked, 'Is that your rifle?'

'Yes.'

'Can I try it? Jay never thinks of letting me shoot. He's a marvellous shot. I've often wondered what it is like to be able to shoot so well. Will you show me how to shoot, Tim?'

'I don't think Mr. Benson would like that.'

'He wouldn't mind. Besides, he's busy trying to fix the car. Please show me.'

She must have picked up the rifle because Timoteo said sharply, alarm in his voice, 'Be careful. It's loaded.'

'Show me.'

'I'm no good at it. I don't think ... I think we should wait for Mr. Benson.'

'You must be better with it than I am. I'm not going to wait, I'm going to try. What do I do?'

'You'd better not.'

'I'm going to.'

Lucy had never fired a rifle. She might kill him. He might kill her. I started forward, then stopped. She was handling him better than I could. This was a risk that might pay off.

I heard him say, 'Wait! You're holding it too loosely. You must hold it hard against your shoulder. The recoil can hurt if you don't. Don't you think we'd better wait ...'

'Like this?'

'Harder against your shoulder. Lucy, please ... you shouldn't ...'

Then the rifle went off. I heard Lucy squeal.

'It hurt!' She was all feminine now.

'You've hit the target!' His high-pitched voice showed his excitement. 'Look!'

'I meant to.' A pause. 'It's not bad, is it for a first shot. Now, you try.'

'I'm no good at it.'

'Tim Savanto! If you can't do better than me you should be ashamed.' She was laughing at him and her voice offered a feminine challenge.

'I don't like guns.'

'I'm going to try again.'

A long pause, then the rifle cracked.

'Oh!'

'You let the sight drop as you fired. I saw it. Let me try.'

'I bet you don't do any better.' There was a friendly jeer in her voice. 'I bet you a nickel. Are you on?'

'I'm on.'

Again there was a long pause, then the rifle barked.

'Oh, you stinker!' Lucy's voice was indignant. 'You said you couldn't shoot! You've stolen my nickel!'

'I'm sorry.' He was actually laughing. 'It was a fluke. Forget the bet! I wouldn't have paid if I had lost... honest.'

I decided it was time to walk in on this scene. I backed off silently, then started to the gallery whistling softly to herald my approach.

I entered the gallery. The moment I walked in, I felt the relaxed atmosphere change. Timoteo was holding the rifle. At the sight of me, he became transfixed. Fear jumped into his eyes and he looked like a dog expecting to be kicked. Lucy was sitting on one of the benches, her face a little flushed, her eyes sparkling. When she saw me, the sparkle died and she looked hopefully at me as if asking for my approval.

'What goes on?' I asked, grinning at her and I was conscious my grin was a little fixed. 'Don't tell me you've been shooting.'

She played up to me, but it didn't quite jell.

'Of course ... and I've hit the target. You're not the only shot around here, Mr. Big-shot. Look ...'

Ignoring Timoteo, I looked at the distant target. There was a hole on the outer ring and another hole by the outer bull.

'Hey ... hey! That's shooting,' I said. 'The inner's a good one!'

'You would say that! You men stick together. That's his. Mine's the outer one.' Even to me the dialogue sounded terrible.

I turned to Timoteo and grinned at him.

'You see? It's not so tough, is it? That's a good start. Go ahead. We have all the ammunition in the world.' I turned to Lucy. 'I've got a gun that'll fit you. Do you want to shoot with him?'

She hesitated, then nodded.

I went over to the gun case, unlocked it and took out a gun that Nick Lewis lent to his lady pupils. I loaded it and handed it to Lucy.

'Hang on a minute, you two. I'll put up new targets. Get off fifty rounds. Okay?'

Timoteo looked like a rabbit about to bolt. I took no notice. Leaving them I went out into the sun and put up new targets.

'Okay, you two,' I called. 'I'm going back to the bungalow. I've letters to write. When I come back, I want to see these targets in bits.'

I grinned towards them, waved to them, then I headed back to the bungalow.

I went straight to the refrigerator and fetched out a can of beer. It was a little early in the day for beer, but I was thirsty ... so what the hell! I carried the beer on to the verandah and sat down. I drank half of it and then lit a cigarette.

I waited.

There was no shooting.

I waited another five minutes ... still no shooting. I finished the beer, threw my half-smoked cigarette away and lit another. The time was now 10.43. Timoteo had been on the range now for four hours and thirty five minutes: during that time he had fired one shot.

What were they playing at? I felt a rush of blood to my head. Lucy must know how important it was to get this slob shooting. Were they sitting there yakking about their parents, their weaknesses, their goddam phobias?

I heaved myself out of the chair, hesitated, then I forced myself to sit down again.

Give her time, I told myself.

Time? Hell! There wasn't any time!

When I had listened to her talking, I was sold she was handling him right. After all, she had got him to hit an inner, but now ... Why didn't she get him started? Why wasn't he shooting?

I sat there for twenty-five minutes: each second I expected to hear a shot: each second dragged by ... no shot.

By now I had worked myself into a vicious mood. I damned him and I damned Lucy. What did they think they were playing at? Exasperated, I got to my feet, threw away my fourth cigarette and started across to the shooting gallery.

I now didn't give a goddam about shaking his nerves. I was fit

48

to kick his backside. I stormed into the dim lean-to like a destructive hurricane.

They weren't there . . . no one was there. The two rifles lay on one of the benches. The distant targets I had set up were untouched. A lizard darted up into the roof, offering the only sign of life.

I walked out of the lean-to, smouldering with fury. Then I saw two sets of footprints in the sand, heading towards the sea.

I stood still, feeling the sun beating down on my head and I looked along the distant beach until I saw them.

They were walking side by side, paddling in the surf, close together: he towering above her, his head bent as if listening to what she was saying. She was carrying her sandals, swinging them as she walked, kicking at the little waves that broke around her ankles. Neither of them looked as if they had a care in the world.

Probably they hadn't, but I had.

Chapter Three

As I stood in the hot sun, I decided there were two things I could do. I could leave them alone or I could go down there, grab him by the scruff of the neck, drag him back to the gallery, slam the rifle in his hands and make him shoot and keep on shooting.

I stood for a long moment watching them, then I contained my rage, turned around and walked back to the bungalow.

My decision to leave them alone was based entirely on what had happened so far. At least, Lucy had got him to hit an inner and I wasn't sure if I could have got him to do that.

To occupy myself and to try to cool down, I sorted out the cans of food and put them away in the store cupboard. I put two bottles of champagne and a dozen cans of beer in the refrigerator.

For lunch, I decided we would have a can of tomato soup,

chickens' breasts, garden peas and fruit salad. I lined up the cans on the table, then I took a beer from the refrigerator and carried it out on to the verandah. I sat down and held on to my temper which was at flash point.

The time was close on 11.36.

From where I sat I couldn't see the beach. The gallery blocked my view. I just sat there thinking about the bond I had buried.

As good a shot as you, Savanto had said. *This is the age of miracles.*

Boy! Some miracle if we were going to continue the way we had started!

After I had smoked three more cigarettes and drunk one more beer, I saw Lucy come into sight around the shooting gallery. She headed towards me, half running, half walking, still holding her sandals in her hand.

She was alone.

I forced myself to sit still.

Why alone?

I waited. She came up a little breathlessly. I could tell by her expression she was scared.

'Hi!' I put down my glass and looked at her. I gave her the look I reserve strictly for goons. 'Did you have a nice paddle?'

She flinched, but she held her ground.

'There was nothing else to do.' I could see she was desperately anxious to explain it all to me. 'When you left, he couldn't even hold the rifle. You frightened the wits out of him.'

'Is that right?' I was ready to explode. 'What's with this boneless creep? Is he weak in the head or something?'

'You frighten him, Jay.'

'You think so?' I sat forward, the blood rising to my face. 'Not half as badly as I intend to frighten him if he goes on acting like a goddam prima donna! Where is he?'

'I told him to stay on the beach until I had talked to you.'

'What's he doing . . . paddling? You realise he should be shooting, don't you? You realise if he doesn't learn to shoot fast we don't get the money? You do realise that, don't you?'

She looked directly at me.

'It's because I do realise it and I do realise how much this means to you that I'm trying to help.'

'You think it's helping to take this goof for a paddle?'

'You wound him up . . . I was unwinding him.'

'What do you mean . . . I wound him up?' My voice was a bark. 'I couldn't have been nicer to the creep! I left him alone with you just so long as he would shoot. So what happens? You take him paddling!'

'You don't seem to realise, Jay, that you frighten people.'

'Now you're going to tell me I frighten you too, aren't you?'

She nodded. Her hands turned into fists. She looked very young, scared and vulnerable.

'Yes. Since this happened you've become someone I don't know. Yes, you frighten me.'

I slapped my hands down hard on my knees. The sound made her start.

'I'm sorry. I don't want to frighten you, but this is important to me. It's important to you. We haven't much time.' I looked around for a way to ease the tension. 'Have a beer?'

'Yes, please.'

I got up and went into the bungalow. I got a beer and poured it into a glass. I took the glass out to her. She was sitting, staring across at the shooting gallery. I gave her the glass, then sat down.

The tension had eased. I watched her drink. Her hand was unsteady. I waited.

'You see, Jay ... he doesn't want to shoot.'

I stared at her.

'He doesn't want to shoot?'

'No.'

'That's fine! That's marvellous! I only want to hear that to make this my perfect day!' I flung my half-smoked cigarette on to the sand. 'So he doesn't want to shoot? Then what the hell is he doing here? His father said he would co-operate! His father said this goof knew the set-up. Now, you tell him he doesn't want to shoot!'

'He's frightened of his father.'

I ran my fingers through my hair.

'But he isn't frightened of you. . . that's something.'

'We are rather alike.'

'You're not! Don't compare yourself with this goon, Lucy. I don't like it.'

'We think alike, Jay.'

I lit another cigarette. I had to do something, otherwise I would have flipped my lid.

'I don't think so, but never mind. Let's get this straight. You've talked to him. Would you say he doesn't give a goddam if his old man loses half a million bucks?'

'He didn't say that.'

'And he also wouldn't give a goddam if we lose fifty thousand bucks?' I leaned forward. Okay, I knew I looked ugly with rage, but who wouldn't flip a lid? 'Well, I do! So does his old man! So he's going to shoot if I have to kick him black and blue! He told his father he would co-operate and that's what he is going to do!'

Lucy put down the glass of half-finished beer. She put her hands on her knees and stared at them as if she were seeing them for the first time.

'You can't make him shoot, Jay, unless he wants to. You know that.'

'So I'll make him want to!'

A long pause, then she looked at me, her clear blue eyes inquiring.

'How will you do that?'

Yeah ... the sixty-four-thousand-dollar question.

'I'll talk to him.' I wasn't even convincing myself. 'I'll make him understand how important this is.'

'He isn't interested in money, Jay. He told me so.'

'I can see that. It's not his money. It's his father's money and my money. Yes, I can see that.'

'Even if it was his, it wouldn't interest him.'

I forced myself to stay calm.

'Now listen, Lucy, I've had punks like him before and I have turned them into riflemen. You go along with them so far, then you have to turn on the heat.' I paused, hesitated, then went on, 'I'm beginning to think Savanto had something when he said it would be better for you not to be here. I want you to pack a bag and go to Paradise City. I'll fix a hotel for you. I want you to stay there for nine days and forget Timoteo. I want you to go right away.'

She looked shocked for a moment, then she stared directly at me.

'You want me to go because you will do things to that boy you would be ashamed to do if I were here. Is that it, Jay?'

That was it, but I wasn't going to admit it.

'Don't talk nonsense. This goof has to be handled. We don't have women around in the Army. I don't want my wife around now. This is important. I want you out of here!'

'I'll get lunch.'

'Lucy! You heard what I said! I want you out of here!'

She got to her feet.

'I'll get lunch,' and she went into the bungalow.

I sat still, on the boil, then I got up and followed her in.

She was looking at the cans lined up on the kitchen table.

'Is this what you want for lunch, Jay?'

'If it's okay with you.'

She began opening the cans.

'After lunch I want you to pack and go.'

'I'm not going.' She poured the soup into a saucepan. Then she paused and looked directly at me. 'I'm not going, Jay.' Her eyes were bright with tears, but her mouth and chin were firm. 'You said: "No matter what, Lucy, I love you. You'll look back on this and you'll forgive me if I've hurt you." That's what you said.' She began to shake a little and she looked quickly out of the open window. 'You're hurting me now, but I'll look back and I'll forgive you.'

That brought me up short. My anger died. I hesitated, then lifted my hands helplessly.

Okay, Lucy, you win. I'm not fighting you or losing you for fifty thousand dollars. So I'll quit. I'll tell Timoteo to get the hell out of here. I'll send the bond back to Savanto. We'll settle for this broken down range and we could still make a success of it. Is that what you want?'

She was looking at the opened can of chickens' breasts.

'This looks nice. Are you hungry?'

'Did you hear what I said?'

A tear ran down her cheek and she flicked it away impatiently.

'Yes, I heard.' She put down the can and now her lips were trembling. 'You may be difficult, Jay, and you may be tough and sometimes unkind, but I do know for sure you're not a quitter.'

I stood looking at her for a long moment. It took me a second or so to realise what she was saying, then I grabbed her, whisked her off her feet and carried her into the bedroom.

'Jay! What are you doing?' She tried to wriggle out of my grip. 'Jay! There's lunch to get ready! Oh, Jay, you mad fool!'

I undid the tops of her jeans and skinned them off her the way you skin a rabbit. I had her standing on the back of her neck before I got them off.

She was protesting, but laughing and crying at the same time.

If I couldn't handle Timoteo Savanto, I could handle my wife.

Hemingway once wrote that when a man and a woman come together the earth moves . . . not often, but sometimes.

Well, the earth moved for us.

*

'Jay . . . you could have given me a baby,' Lucy said.

I opened my eyes and stared up at the ceiling with its patterns of sunlight, then I turned over on my side to look at her.

'Would you like that?' I asked.

'Yes. Would you?'

'I guess. I'd teach the little bastard to shoot.'

'It could be a girl.'

I grinned at her.

'Then you could teach her to be nice, kind, understanding and as sexy as you are.'

We looked at each other.

'I'm sorry, honey. I got worked up. Truly, I'm sorry.'

She touched my hand.

'It's all right, Jay . . . honest.'

From her smile I knew it was all right.

'You don't really think we made a kid?' I asked.

She giggled.

'That's how babies are made. We could have.'

She slid off the bed and struggled into her jeans.

'Look at the time!'

It was 12.43.

I got off the bed and found my slacks.

'I'll get him. You get lunch.'

'No . . . leave him. He told me he doesn't have lunch. He only eats once a day.'

I shrugged, thinking: a real goon.

'Well, okay, but remember I eat three times a day.'

'As if I could forget.'

She ran off into he kitchen.

I went out on to the verandah. Making love the way we had had relaxed me. I felt I had solved a problem with Lucy, but I still had to solve the problem with Timoteo.

After lunch we took our coffee out on the verandah.

'What will you do, Jay?'

'Go down there and talk to him. It's okay, Lucy, I'll handle him with kid gloves. Did you get around to calling our six pupils?'

She flushed.

'I – I forgot.'

'It doesn't matter. The phone's on the blink.'

She looked questioningly at me.

'What's the matter with it?'

'The same as the car. We're cut off for nine days. Raimundo is in charge of security.'

'This is crazy!'

'There it is. I guess . . .'

I saw she wasn't listening. She had stiffened and was looking beyond me and the scared look was back in her eyes.

I looked around.

Raimundo was leaning against one of the uprights of the verandah. His eyes were screwed up against the sun. He was looking directly at me.

I finished my coffee, taking my time, then I asked him what he wanted.

'Can I talk to you?' He sounded polite and he wasn't grinning.

'Go ahead.'

He glanced at Lucy.

'You coming over to the gallery?'

I got to my feet.

'I'll get to work,' I said, smiling at Lucy. 'See you.'

I left the shade of the verandah and started off towards the gallery. Raimundo fell into step beside me. We walked in silence until we reached the gallery.

'What's on your mind?' I asked.

'It's not what's on my mind. It's what's on yours. Why isn't he shooting?'

'Look, glamour-boy, you take care of security and I'll take care of the shooting . . . right?'

His eyes were like points of steel now.

'It's time you came down to earth, soldier. You don't seem to know what you've walked into.'

'You're flapping with your mouth again. Beat it!' I said. 'I have a job to do and you have a job to do. I do my job my way: you do yours your way. Now, dust!'

He walked into the lean-to and sat on one of the benches. I hesitated, then joined him.

'Come on . . . beat it!' I snapped.

He looked up at me.

'Are you having trouble with Timoteo?'

'Up on the legs and dust.'

'Because if you are I can fix it. That's why I'm here.'

'Is it? I thought you were here to take care of the security.'

'That and Timoteo.'

Then I remembered what Savanto had said. *Two of my men will be arriving tomorrow with Timoteo. They will look after*

55

security, and they will also look after Timoteo if he gets difficult.

I sat down on the opposite bench. I thought for a moment, then shrugged.

'I guess I'm having trouble with him,' I said. 'He doesn't want to shoot.'

'Okay. Why didn't you say so? I'll fix it.'

The confidence in his voice made me stare at him.

'I didn't ask you to fix it. What's the matter with him?'

Raimundo sneered.

'Just a big yellow streak ... that's all. You and Mrs. Benson have now been with him since 06.00. He has fired off only two shots. Okay, now I'll talk to him.'

'What do you tell him?'

A sneering smile showed his white teeth.

'That's between Timoteo and myself, soldier.'

'I'll talk to him first. This morning he was so jumpy he couldn't even hold the rifle. He's had time to calm down. I'll talk to him. If it doesn't work, then you talk to him.'

'Okay. I'll give you two hours.'

'You'll give me nothing! I'll tell you when to talk to him ... understand?'

He regarded me with a sneering pity that tempted me to hit him.

'Man! Do you sound off! Maybe, instead of talking to him, I'd better talk to you.' He sat back and stabbed his forefinger in my direction. 'You don't know it yet, but you're in a jam. You've got to deliver or else. What you have to get into your thick skull is this set-up isn't a game. That yellow slob has got to shoot and it's your job to make him shoot! If you flop, then you'll not only lose the money Mr. Savanto's promised you, but you will be in personal trouble!'

I felt blood rush to my face.

'Are you threatening me?'

'No. I don't threaten anyone ... I deliver messages.' He stared at me with his bleak, black eyes. 'That's the message Mr. Savanto told me to deliver to you. Remember this: this isn't a game. You're being well paid. You deliver or you'll be in trouble.' He stood up. 'Don't bust an artery over me. I'm just the messenger boy.' He balanced himself on his feet, his hands hanging loosely and I could see he was ready to take and to give a punch. 'You got the message, soldier?'

'Get my phone connected,' I said. 'I'll talk to Savanto. I'm going to tell him I want you off the scene.'

He grinned.

'Wouldn't you like that? If he isn't shooting by 16.00, I'll talk to him.'

He walked off. When he was some fifty yards from me, he began to sing.

With his looks and his voice he was a TV natural.

*

I found Timoteo sitting under a palm tree, staring out to sea. His long legs were drawn up so that his chin was resting on his knees; his big hands hung slackly between his drawn-up legs.

I paused to watch him. I stood there in the hot sun for perhaps a minute. During that time, he didn't move. He looked as if he were in a trance.

So I had to teach this zombie to shoot! In the past, I had had some crummy material through my hands, but none so crummy as this sad sack.

I had promised Lucy I would handle him with kid gloves. My instinct was to kick him to his feet and then kick him to the gallery. I waited another minute while I mentally put on my kid gloves, then I approached him. It wasn't until my shadow fell across his big feet that he became aware I was with him.

He reacted as if someone had goosed him with a hot iron. He sprang to his feet and looked around in panic for a way of escape.

'Hi, Tim,' I said. 'Sorry if I startled you. You were miles away.'

He was wearing the sun goggles again. I had to restrain myself from jerking them off his face and smashing them.

'For the love of mike, sit down.' I grinned at him. 'The way you act, I'm beginning to think you don't like me.'

I sat in the shade. He still stood there, looking as if he were going to bolt, the vein in his temple pounding.

'Can't you sit down?'

He gulped, hesitated, then slowly and reluctantly folded himself about five feet from me. He drew up his long legs and stared fixedly out to sea.

'I want to talk to you,' I said. 'Lucy's convinced me from the moment we met we got off on the wrong foot. You're due an explanation. You see, Tim, I'm a one time Army instructor. In the Army, things have to get done fast. There's no time to take personalities into consideration, and without meaning to I have got you feeling hostile towards me.'

I waited for him to say something, but he didn't. He continued to hide behind the goggles and look towards the sea.

I rubbed the back of my neck and contained my impatience. I had promised Lucy to handle him with kid gloves, so I was going to.

'Your father wants you to become a crack shot. He wants to win an important, big money bet. You know about that. He made a mistake making the bet, but we all make mistakes sometime or other. I guess because you're his son, you'll want to get him out of the mess he's in.' Again I eyed the profile: again no response. 'He picked on me to help you. I don't know if he told you, but he is offering me fifty thousand dollars to make you a good shot in nine days. With your co-operation, this is possible.' Again no response. I went on, 'You've been here a few hours and you've seen this place. It's in a mess. I've sunk all the money I got from the Army into it. Maybe I've made a mistake. What I need is extra capital to give this dump a shot in the arm. Your father will give me the capital if – only if – I turn you into a good shot. With this capital, Lucy and I can make a success of the range.'

I looked at him. He continued to stare out to sea. He might have been stone deaf for all the impact I was making on him.

I sat for a long minute, resisting the urge to get up and kick the arse off him.

'You've already talked to Lucy,' I said, making my final appeal. 'She tells me you two think alike. Getting capital to put this place on its feet is as important to her as it is to me. What I'm trying to say, Tim, is now I've explained the set-up to you, can I rely on your co-operation? Will you help us by letting me help you?'

I waited, watching him. He just sat there, but his big hands had turned into fists. Well, at least he was showing signs of being alive.

I waited. I had said all I had to say. If he didn't respond, then I had made up my mind to give him the Army treatment.

Finally, just when I was about to start bawling at him, he began to unwind like a mechanical figure and he climbed to his feet. He hesitated, not looking at me, then with slow, dragging steps, he started towards the shooting gallery.

When he had disappeared into the lean-to, I got up and went after him.

I found him standing by his rifle. He had taken off the goggles and he looked as miserable and as animated as a drowned cat.

I loaded the rifle.

'Go ahead, Tim,' I said. 'Take it nice and easy. We have all the afternoon. I want you to get as close to the bull as you can. Don't get fussed if you don't make good shooting: that'll come. Okay?'

He took the rifle, went over to the shooting stand and began firing.

I let him loose off six shots. He didn't even clip the target.

'Okay, Tim ... hold it.' I got out the tripod that Nick Lewis used to use for his most hopeless women pupils. I fixed it up, screwed the rifle to it, lined up the sight, then stepped back. 'Just keep shooting.' With the tripod he couldn't miss. I thought maybe when he saw his grouping, he might get ambitious. I let him fire off twenty rounds during which time he cut the bull out of the target.

'That's shooting, but it's only because the gun is rock steady.' I took the gun off the tripod. 'Now take it dead slow. I only want you to shoot when you're sure you're on target. If it takes an hour to fire six rounds that's okay with me.'

With sweat running down his face, he hung on to the rifle for so long I thought he had become paralysed, then finally he fired. We had a new target now. He got an outer. Well, at least he was hitting something.

After an hour, he had managed to place six shots around the outer ring and in a group. This was better progress than I had hoped for. All the time he was shooting, he remained silent. He was so tense I imagined I could hear his muscles creaking. Although I wanted to keep him at it, I knew this wouldn't help.

'Okay, Tim, let's knock it off. I've got a thirst on me that would slay a camel. Let's go over to the bungalow and show Lucy what you've been doing.'

He lowered the rifle the way Hercules must have lowered the world. I went down the sand and took off his two targets and then joined him.

'How do you feel about it, Tim? It's not so hard, is it?'

'No.'

He put his sun goggles on again and I was shut out.

As we approached the bungalow, I saw Lucy was painting. She was on a ladder, doing the gutter. Already the bungalow looked pretty smart.

'Hi, Lucy ... beer,' I called.

She looked down and waved her paint brush, smiling.

'Get it yourself, helpless. I'm busy.'

'Come on down. I want you to see what Tim's been doing.'

'Suppose Tim comes on up and finishes this gutter. It's killing me!'

He started forward like a greyhound released from the trap. He was at the bottom of the ladder before I got moving.

I heard him say, 'I'll be glad to do it. It's too hard for you, Lucy.'

I hung back as she came down the ladder and gave him the brush and the pot of paint. As he climbed the ladder she joined me.

We walked together into the kitchen.

'The trouble with him is he's simple minded,' I said as I took two cans of beer from the refrigerator.

'How did he shoot?'

I waved to the two targets on the table, then zipped open one of the cans of beer. I took a long pull from the can as she studied the targets.

'This is good, isn't it?'

'Well, it's a start.'

She looked quickly at me.

'Thank you for being kind to him, Jay. He needs kindness.'

She went out carrying a can of beer. I hesitated, then shrugged. I was sweating. When I had finished the beer, I went into the bedroom, stripped off and took a shower. I didn't hurry. Thirty minutes later, I came out on to the verandah.

Lucy was finishing off the gutter. Timoteo wasn't around.

'Where is he?'

Lucy looked down from the top of the ladder.

'He's gone back to the gallery.'

'He has? What's this . . . sudden enthusiasm?'

I heard the crack of the rifle.

'I asked him to go back.'

'Thanks, Lucy. I'll get over there.'

'No, don't. Leave him alone. Let him shoot on his own. We have a bet on.'

I looked up at her. I could see she was anxious and bothered.

'You betted him he could do better?'

'Yes.' She slapped on more paint. 'He needs that sort of encouragement.'

I began to get it.

'You mean he's fallen for you. Is that it?'

'I guess so. You don't mind, do you, Jay?'

I grinned a little uneasily.

'So long as you haven't fallen for him.'

She flushed and looked away.

'Of course not!'

All the time we were talking the rifle was firing ... slow: five or six shots every three minutes. I could imagine him shooting as if his life depended on it.

Then I saw Raimundo coming across the sand. He was carrying a long cardboard box in his hand, swinging it and slapping his thigh with it as he walked.

I waited, aware that Lucy, high up on the ladder, had also stopped painting.

He came up, taking his time, his eyes first going to Lucy, then shifting to me.

'So you've got him shooting.' he said.

'What do you want?'

'Something from Mr. Savanto ... special delivery. Goon has to shoot with it ... orders.' He offered me the box.

'What is it?'

'Take a look, soldier. You've got eyes.' He stared up at Lucy, then he gave me his jeering smile, turned around and walked off with that insolent lounging movement that made me long to kick him.

As I began to open the box, Lucy scrambled down the ladder and joined me.

'What is it, Jay?'

I squatted on the sand as I took off the lid. There was a slip of paper on top of some foam packing. The note was type-written:

Timoteo will shoot with these two attachments. See to it, please.   A.S.

'What is it?' Lucy repeated, peering over my shoulder.

'A telescopic sight. This is a silencer. They are both highly sophisticated ... both cost the earth.'

'But why?'

'The telescopic sight will make it much easier for him to hit a bull. When Savanto first talked to me I wondered about a telescopic sight, but I didn't imagine it would come within the rules of his bet.' I turned the sight over in my hands. 'He can't fail to shoot well with this.'

'But why a silencer?'

I shrugged. I was asking myself the same question.

'I don't know.' I stood up. 'The silencer will make it a little more tricky for him. I'll get these two attachments fitted to the rifle right away before he gets used to the rifle as it is.'

'All this worries me, Jay.'

'Oh, come on, Lucy,' I said a little impatiently. 'There's nothing to get worried about.'

Leaving her, I walked over to the gallery. He was there, the rifle against his shoulder, his face against the shoulder of the gun, his shirt black with sweat. As I came in, he fired again. I looked beyond him at the distant target. He had another set of holes topside of the inner ring. He was still off the bull, but at least he was still grouping.

'Hi, Tim,' I said. 'We've got the answer to your problem. Look at this.'

He started like he had received an electric shock and dropped the rifle. He spun around, gaped at me, flinched, then stepped back where he had no room to step back, cannoned off the shooting rest.

'For God's sake!' I was as startled as he by this exhibition of nerves. 'Can't you relax? Look at this.'

He continued to gape at me, his eyes wild, his expression dazed.

'Your father sent this over. It'll help you more than I can.'

As he still remained paralysed, I picked up the rifle and took it over to one of the benches. I sat down. It took me a couple of minutes to clip on the sight and to screw on the silencer.

I looked at him. He was staring at the rifle like you might stare at a snake that had dropped into your bath.

What a goon! I thought. To give him time to straighten himself out, I went over to the shooting rest and sighted through the telescopic sight at the target. It was as if I could stretch out my arm and put my finger right on the bull. In my time, I had handled a lot of telescopic sights, but nothing as good as this one.

'Take a look through this, Tim,' I said, turning.

The sight of him as he stood in the dimly lit lean-to set my nerves tingling. He looked as if he had gone out of his mind. There was a wild, crazy look in his eyes: his mouth was working: the muscles in his neck were standing out like knotted ropes and he began hissing through his clenched teeth.

'Hey! Tim!' I shouted. 'What's the matter?'

He came at me with two quick shuffling strides. I was handicapped by the rifle I was holding. His fist slammed against the side of my head with the force of a steam hammer. My knees buckled, then dimly I saw his fist coming again towards my face. There was nothing I could do about it. I felt the shock, then a white flash of light scorched my eyes, then nothing.

*

I became aware of the sound of the sea pounding on the beach. Then I became aware my jaw was aching. The ache reminded me of the fist flashing towards my face. I shook my head, grunted and sat up. This wasn't the first time I had taken a punch, but I couldn't remember taking a harder one.

I looked around. I was on my own. I fingered the swelling on my jaw, winced, then levered myself to my feet.

The rifle with its telescopic sight and its silencer lay on the sand. I looked at it, continued to rub my jaw, coaxing my mind to work.

Then I heard a sound. Raimundo appeared in the doorway. He propped himself up against one of the posts of the lean-to and regarded me. His eyes were bored; a cigarette burned between his fingers.

I picked up the rifle and laid it carefully on one of the benches.

'For a guy who's getting paid fifty thousand bucks, you certainly are some flop,' he said.

'That's right.' I sat down, pushing the rifle along the bench to give me room. 'Yeah, I guess that's fair criticism.' I was still a little dizzy in the head. 'What's with this jerk? Is he crazy?'

Raimundo flicked ash off his cigarette.

'He's nervous.'

'Just nervous, huh?' I tried my teeth carefully with my tongue. None of them seemed loose. 'He's quite a puncher, isn't he?'

'You could call him that.'

'What makes him nervous?'

Raimundo flicked more ash off his cigarette.

'He has his troubles. Don't we all?'

'He's more than nervous. He has a couple of screws loose and you know it.'

Raimundo shrugged.

'Where is he?'

'Nick's taking care of him.'

I rubbed my jaw. It didn't help.

'Get my phone connected. I'm going to talk to his father.'

'I bet.' Raimundo sneered. 'Right now, Mr. Savanto doesn't want to talk to you, soldier. When he does talk to you, he'll want to hear the goon can shoot. He isn't interested in your problems. He pays. You deliver.'

I got to my feet. 'Then I'll talk to Timoteo.'

Raimundo shook his head.

'You've had your chance. You don't know how to handle him. He doesn't react to the soft approach. From now on, I'm handling him and tell your wife to lay off the palsy-walsy act. You be here at 09.00 tomorrow. Goon will be here, ready to shoot.'

Why should I care? I reasoned to myself. I was being paid to teach him to shoot not to act as a mental nurse.

'Suits me.'

I unclipped the telescopic sight, ran a rag over it, unscrewed the silencer and put it and the sight into the box. I put the rifle back in its case and the box and the rifle case into the gun rack.

'Nine tomorrow, then?'

'That's it, soldier.'

I left the gallery and started across the hot sand to the bungalow. The time was 19.34.

Lucy had finished painting. As I walked into the living-room, I heard the shower going. I went to the liquor cabinet, took out a bottle of scotch and poured a slug. I drank it neat, then went into the bedroom.

Lucy came out of the shower, a towel wrapped around her.

'Did you bring Tim with you?' she asked, darting to the closet to find a dress.

'No. Raimundo is taking care of him. You finished with the shower?'

The note in my voice made her turn quickly. She saw the bruise and the swelling on my face.

'What happened? Your face!'

I stripped off my shirt.

'It's nothing, honey.'

'But what happened?'

I told her.

'He's as nutty as a fruit cake,' I said as I kicked off my shoes. 'Our luck . . . to get landed with him.'

She held the towel around her as she stared at me.

'I can't believe it. He hit you!'

I took off my slacks.

'He carries quite a punch. Anyway, what's it matter? In the state he was in he'd have hit his own father.'

I went into the shower. After standing under the cold water

for some minutes, I felt more relaxed. I dried off and came back into the bedroom.

Lucy had put on a dress. She sat on the bed and watched me while I threw on slacks and shirt.

'Why did he hit you, Jay?'

'He was worked up. I don't know. He looked as if he were going to throw a fit.'

'But what did you do to him?'

'I did nothing to him!' I found I was shouting at her. I throttled back. 'I'm sorry, Lucy. I'm getting worked up myself. What's for supper?'

'There's something terribly wrong. He wouldn't hit anyone. This worries me.'

'Well, he hit me.' I tried to grin, but it didn't come off. 'He's neurotic. Let's forget him. I've had him in my hair all day. What's for supper?'

She got up.

'Would you like eggs and ham or do you want something more fancy?' Her voice was unsteady and her eyes cloudy.

'Eggs and ham would be fine. Come on . . . I'll help.'

We went into the kitchen and I sat on the table while she got the eggs from the refrigerator.

'Is he coming to sleep here?'

'I don't think so. I hope not.' I watched her as she set the frying pan on the stove. 'Now look, Lucy, don't get worked up. He has a screw loose. I'm sure of it. I should have let Raimundo handle him from the start. We made the mistake of being soft with him. Raimundo says he starts shooting tomorrow morning. That's all I want to hear. Let's forget him for tonight. I've had enough of him.'

She turned to face me.

'He's desperately frightened.'

'You call it one thing. I call it another. Let's forget him for God's sake!'

'Yes, Jay.'

I watched her break the eggs into the hot fat.

'You've forgotten the ham.'

She flushed and began to dither. She turned off the gas and put on the grill.

'That's not a hot idea, is it?'

She started shaking.

'Oh, Jay, I'm so worried. What does all this mean?'

'You're making a mess of our dinner,' I said. 'Come on, Lucy, forget him!'

I left her and went out on to the verandah. Maybe I was being unkind, but I had had enough of Timoteo Savanto and my jaw ached.

After a while, she brought out two plates. The eggs were like bullets and the ham soggy. While we ate, I told her about the bond in the biscuit box and where I had buried it.

'Are you listening, Lucy? This is important.'

'Yes.'

'It's a lot of money. I'd look a dope if it were stolen.'

'Yes.'

We left most of the food on our plates.

'I'm sorry, Jay. It was badly cooked.'

'I've eaten worse.' I lit a cigarette. 'Anything on TV?'

'I don't know . . . I haven't looked.'

I went inside to get the TV Guide. There was a six-year-old Western with Burt Lancaster. My jaw was now beginning to ache in earnest. I turned the set on.

Lucy took the plates into the kitchen. I sat down and watched the antics on the screen. Men rode down the mountains in a cascade of falling rocks and dust. They killed each other with guns and knives. I held my throbbing jaw and watched.

Later, Lucy came and sat near me. She didn't look at the screen. She sat still, looking out of the open window as the darkness slowly settled over the beach and the sea.

The film finished with a massacre as most Westerns do. As the credit titles came up, I switched off.

'Let's go to bed.'

'Is it all right to leave everything open?'

I knew she was thinking of Raimundo.

'Why not? I'm here.'

We went into the bedroom. We took turns in the bathroom and then we lay on the bed with the view of the moon lighting the sea and the palms outlined against the dark sky.

My jaw still throbbed, but I was being brave about it.

'What's going to happen tomorrow, Jay?' she asked out of the darkness and in a small voice.

I slid my arm around her and pulled her to me.

'Why worry about tomorrow?' I turned her so she could see over my shoulder as I held her. 'Look at the moon.'

I was at the gallery a few minutes to nine o'clock and I didn't have to wait long. As the minute hand of my watch moved on to the hour, I saw Raimundo and Timoteo coming across the sand.

I watched them come. Raimundo walked with his usual swagger. Timoteo, his head bent, shuffled along, a step or two in the rear. He was wearing his sun goggles and his shirt was already sticking to him.

I had the rifle ready. I didn't know what to expect and I wasn't in a relaxed frame of mind. My jaw was sore and the bruise was turning black. I still couldn't believe a slob like Timoteo could have punched that hard.

When they were within ten yards of me, Raimundo said something to Timoteo who stopped short and stood like an ox waiting for the yoke. Raimundo joined me.

'Take him,' he said. 'He'll do what you tell him. Get him shooting, soldier. Don't chat him up. Just get him shooting.'

I beckoned to Timoteo. I decided to treat him like an Army recruit: nothing personal and all business.

Without looking at me, he walked slowly and heavy-footed into the lean-to and stopped, looking helplessly at the distant targets.

'Get those goggles off!' I barked.

He flinched, but took them off. As he was about to put them in his shirt pocket, Raimundo moved forward.

'I'll have them.'

Timoteo hesitated then handed them over. Raimundo took them, paused while he looked at Timoteo, then he dropped the goggles on the sand and trod on them. I wouldn't have done that, but I was glad it was done. The goggles were to this goon as a rag is to a kid who thumb-sucks.

'The rifle is loaded,' I said. 'Get shooting.'

He took the rifle. There was a dumb, broken look on his face. I suddenly thought: suppose he turns the rifle on me or Raimundo? What a couple of jerks we'd look! Seeing the way he stood, wavering, the rifle in his hands, brought me out in a sudden cold sweat, but it was all right. I could see the thought had never entered his head. He turned and went to the shooting rest.

This was the first time he had looked through the telescopic sight. I saw his back stiffen as the target seemed to leap at him.

'Take your time,' I said in my instructor's voice. 'Get the cross wires on the bull. Don't pull the trigger; squeeze it.' I gave him a couple of seconds to get ready. 'Shoot when you want to.'

Another couple of seconds crawled by, then the rifle banged.

Both Raimundo and I looked towards the target. He had hit the bull dead centre.

'Good shot,' I said. 'That's the way. Now keep on shooting.'

With that telescopic sight, unless you had Parkinson's disease, you couldn't fail to hit a bull, but with his next ten shots he only hit the bull twice.

I kept him at it: reloading for him, handing the rifle back without looking at him.

Raimundo sat on one of the benches and smoked. After the first shot, he didn't bother to look at the target, but he sat there and I knew his presence was keeping Timoteo shooting.

After an hour, and after he had scored ten bulls out of sixty shots, I said, 'Okay . . . break it off.' I turned to Raimundo.

'Take him for a walk. I want him back in an hour,' and I walked out and headed towards the bungalow.

Lucy was busy scraping the paint off the front door. She paused in her work and looked inquiringly up at me.

'He's taking time off,' I said. 'How are you getting on? I have an hour. I'll give a hand.'

'It's all right. I like doing it.' She stood up. 'Do you want a beer?'

'It's too early.' I moved to one of our crummy sling chairs on the verandah and sat down. She joined me.

'I didn't hear any shooting.'

'He's using the silencer. He's shooting . . . not bad.'

'But how is he?'

'He's okay. He's shooting. That's all we need worry about.'

'Is that man with him?'

'Raimundo? Oh, sure. He's sitting in on the session. He's the oil that makes the goon function.'

'Oh, Jay! Haven't you any heart? Can't you see this boy is frightened to death?' She wrung her hands. 'Can't you see this awful man is terrifying him into shooting?'

I rubbed the back of my neck while I restrained my impatience.

'I couldn't talk him into shooting. You couldn't mother him into shooting. Okay, Raimundo is scaring him into shooting. He's got to shoot. I'm being paid fifty thousand dollars to get him to shoot so . . .'

She got up abruptly and went into the bungalow.

So we were going to start this all over again, I thought. I sat there for five minutes, feeling the ache in my jaw, then I got up, kicked the chair away and walked into the living-room.

She was sitting on a stool, facing the empty fireplace, her clenched fists against her face.

'Lucy, will you please try to be helpful,' I said. 'It's tough enough to have this nut in my hair without you going neurotic on me. This is important to us! I'm trying to earn...'

'Oh, stop it!' Her voice was shrill and her eyes a little wild. 'I'm not neurotic! You're just mad about money! Can't you see...?'

'Lucy!' My bark stopped her dead. An Army voice when it is pitched right can stop a clock. 'What's with it between you and this goon? Are you falling for him? Have you fallen for him?'

Her face crimson, her eyes shocked, she stared at me.

'What are you saying?'

'I'm asking you. What's all this protective stuff with this creep? What's he mean to you?'

'He's a human being! He's frightened! I'm sorry for him. That's what he means to me!'

'Well, okay ... just stay sorry for him, but nothing else. I asked you, Lucy, to keep out of this. Please stop throwing spanners in the works! I have enough to handle without you getting protective.'

'Money means everything to you, doesn't it?'

'We're not talking about money! We're talking about this goon!'

'To you, it's the same thing.'

'I'm being paid to teach him to shoot. That's what I'm trying to do!'

'He doesn't want to shoot ... he told me.'

I held on to the explosion that was building up in me.

'What he told you and what he is going to do are two different things. Will you please leave this to me?'

'Why don't you find out why he doesn't want to shoot? Why don't you start treating him like a human being? Why do you let a thug dictate to you and to him?' She jumped to her feet. 'I can tell you! All you think about is the money you will make!'

'Is that something to be ashamed of?'

'I think it is.'

I touched my aching jaw. It looked to me as if we were back on square A.

'I'm sorry you feel this way about it, Lucy,' I said. 'You've made your point. This is a job I'm going through with. I'm asking you to stick with it for another eight days.' I didn't wait for her to make a come-back, I left her and returned to the shooting gallery.

I would have to get Timoteo shooting soon at moving targets. Nick Lewis had an antiquated machine which I had inherited. Sometimes it worked ... sometimes it didn't. It was run by a small electric motor which turned cogs which turned a conveyor belt. Attached to the belt were six screw bolts. On the bolts you could fix decoy birds, targets, beer cans and so on. The motor could be speeded up if it felt like speeding up or it could take the targets along at a snail's pace.

I was working on the machine when Raimundo and Timoteo came in.

'We'll keep to target shooting for today,' I said to Timoteo as I handed him the rifle. 'Tomorrow, we'll try a moving target.'

I wasn't sure if he had heard me. He didn't look as if he had, but I was past caring. His despairing, broken down look bored me.

He shot until noon. His score of bulls was increasing. A few minutes after noon, his concentration began slipping and I could see it was time to stop.

I turned to Raimundo who was lighting yet another cigarette.

'I'll take him to the bungalow and feed him. We'll start again at 14.00.'

Raimundo got to his feet.

'I'll feed him, soldier. He stays with me. Come on, Mr. Savanto, let's go see what Nick's cooked up for us.' He cocked a mocking eye at me. 'I'll have him here at 14.00.'

That suited me. The less I had to do with this goon the better I liked it.

I watched them walk off towards the line of distant palm trees, then I went back to the bungalow.

The next three days are of no interest to record: they followed the same pattern. Raimundo delivered Timoteo to the gallery at nine o'clock every morning, took him away to eat at noon, brought him back at 14.00 and took him away at 19.00. During this time Timoteo shot, used up a lot of ammunition, did what he was told, often badly and sometimes better than badly.

I had to contain my impatience and control my temper when he started on the moving targets. He either shot ahead or behind, but after some hours he began to hit a few beer cans that were being conveyed along at the slowest speed the machine would operate at.

Lucy continued to paint the bungalow. She no longer asked about Timoteo. She had no chance of seeing him anyway. Our personal feelings for each other had suffered a knock. We were both too goddam polite to each other, and we had long minutes of complete silence that hadn't come into our lives before.

I knew she was worried sick and she was hurt, but I kept telling myself that when this was over it would be forgotten and we would get together again as before.

After the third day I became more aware that time was running out and I began to turn on the heat. It wasn't good enough for Timoteo to hit two beer cans out of five as they crept along the belt. He had to sharpen up his ideas.

I gave the wheels driving the belt some machine oil and advanced the motor.

The cans jolted along at three times their previous speed. He fired off forty shots without hitting a can.

Exasperated, I shouted at him, 'Shoot ahead! All the time you're shooting behind!'

I didn't believe anyone could sweat the way he sweated. He was trying all right, but his reflexes were those of a cripple.

He kept shooting, kept missing, and I could see by his desperate expression he was becoming hysterical.

'Okay, stop.' I turned to Raimundo. 'Take him away. Let him relax.' I switched off the motor. 'I've had enough of him for today.'

Raimundo stared at me, his black eyes evil.

'He hasn't time to relax, soldier. Mr. Savanto is coming to check on him the day after tomorrow. You'll be the one who'll need to relax if he isn't doing better than this.'

I would have to be deaf not to catch the threat in his voice. So I kept him shooting until dusk, but it was a waste of ammunition. He hit three of the beer cans out of a hundred shots. By then he was in no condition even to hold the rifle.

'That's it,' I said in disgust. 'He can't shoot any more. Take him away.'

I was sweating myself. If Savanto was coming in forty-eight hours and expected to see something for his money, time was certainly running against me.

When they had gone I returned to the bungalow. I could smell onions frying. I found Lucy in the kitchen, preparing a curry

. . . one of my favourite meals and the one thing she could cook well.

'Hi!'

She looked over her shoulder and gave me a ghost of a smile.

'Through for the day?'

'Yeah, I'll take a shower.'

'It'll be ready in twenty minutes.'

'It smells good.'

She nodded and turned back to the stove. I eyed her for a brief moment, feeling depressed and wanting to touch her, but there was no invitation to touch her in that stiff slim back.

It'll work out, I told myself. It's got to work out.

After the shower, I put on fresh slacks and a shirt.

We had dinner. The curry was good: just the way I liked it, but I didn't have much appetite: nor did she.

'He's bogged down on the moving target,' I said. 'It's going to be a miracle if I ever make this sonofabitch shoot.'

She moved the food about on her plate with her fork. She didn't say anything.

'His father is coming to check on his progress the day after tomorrow.'

That got a reaction. She looked up, her eyes widening.

'Is he?'

'Yes. I wish I hadn't taken this job, Lucy.'

'You still have six days.' She put down her fork. 'You can't expect to make all this money without working for it. That's what you said, wasn't it?'

'That's what I said.'

Then followed another of our long, depressing silences.

'I forgot to tell you,' she said. 'Colonel Forsythe came for his lesson. I told him the school was closed.'

'Did he take it all right?' I couldn't care less about Colonel Forsythe or any of my other pupils.

'Yes.'

Again a long silence.

'I guess it's too hot to eat,' I said and pushed my plate away.

She had scarcely eaten anything.

Without looking at me, she got up from the table and went out onto the verandah. From force of habit, I turned on the TV set. A blonde with a mouth as big as a bucket was yelling about love. I turned the set off.

Through the open window, I saw Lucy walking towards the sea. I hesitated for a moment, then went after her.

Side by side, and in silence, we walked along the deserted beach.

After a while, I reached for her hand, but she didn't reach for mine.

*

By lunch-time the next day, I knew there was going to be no miracle.

For three solid hours, Timoteo fired at the moving cans, using up ammunition and hitting none of them. He was trying all right, but his reflexes seemed to be paralysed. Even when I slowed the moving targets down again to a crawl he still couldn't hit them.

Finally, I took the rifle out of his sweating hands.

'Sit down, Tim,' I said. 'Let's talk.'

He stood there, his head lowered, his face grey and drawn. He looked like a bull with the pics in, waiting for the blade.

'Tim!' I barked at him. 'Sit down! I want to talk to you!'

The snap in my voice brought his head up. The despair and the hate in his eyes shocked me. Then he turned and moving like a zombie, he walked out of the gallery and into the hot sunshine. He hesitated for a moment, then set off with his slow, shambling stride towards the distant palm trees.

I looked at Raimundo who was sitting on one of the benches, watching me.

'That's it,' I said. 'I'm quitting. I know when I'm licked. He'll never make it. I want to talk to your boss.'

Raimundo flicked his cigarette away.

'Yeah, it's time to talk to the boss.' He stood up. 'We'll go and talk to him now. I'll fix your car.'

I knew this was the end of my dream of owning fifty thousand dollars and I realised with a sense of surprise, I didn't care. No money was worth what I had gone through during the past days. If I had had only Timoteo to handle I might have had some regrets even though I had learned the hard way he was beyond teaching, but it wasn't only Timoteo. Because I had been hypnotised by the thought of all that money, I was spoiling my marriage.

'I'll meet you at the bungalow,' I said.

I found Lucy in the kitchen, preparing the lunch.

'I'm seeing Savanto now. I'm returning the money. In a few hours we will be rid of them all,' I said, coming to rest by her side.

She stiffened, staring at me.

'What happened?'

'I suddenly realised I need this job like I need a hole in the head,' I said quietly. 'He'll never learn to shoot. I'm quitting, and we're going back to square A.' I grinned at her. 'I won't be long, honey, I'm getting the money.'

I went out through the back door, dug up the biscuit box and took out the bond. Before, I had handled it with reverence, now I stuffed it into my hip pocket. It was nothing to me but a piece of paper.

As I returned to the kitchen, through the window, I saw the Volkswagen pull up.

'I'll be back in a couple of hours,' I said. 'Wait for me?'

'Yes.'

There was a flat note in her voice and uneasiness in her eyes. Then she went on, 'Oh, Jay! Why didn't you realise this before?'

Raimundo, sitting in the driving seat, blared the horn.

'We'll talk about it. I've got to go. Wait for me.'

There was something in the way she was holding herself that warned me not to touch her. I blew her a kiss and then went out and got in the Volkswagen.

We drove in silence along Highway 1, heading towards Paradise City. Raimundo drove well and as fast as the car could make it.

I turned over in my mind what I was going to say to Savanto. I remembered Raimundo's words: *If you flop, then you are not only going to lose the money, but you will be in personal trouble.*

A cheap gangster's bluff?

I looked at him. His handsome profile gave away nothing of his thoughts, if he was thinking: a hard, cruel face: a man to take seriously.

Personal trouble?

I felt a spasm of uneasiness.

This is the age of miracles, Savanto had said.

But within reason. You had to have talent and a lot of willingness and Timoteo had neither. He did try. I had to admit that, so perhaps unwillingness was unfair. He had some deep mental block that prevented him from shooting. I remembered Lucy had urged me to ask him why he didn't want to shoot. I had never got around to asking him, but I doubted if he would have told me if I had bothered to ask. Maybe, I thought, I should have made the effort, but I was a shooting instructor, not a psychologist.

I wasn't aching to talk to Savanto. He would blame me for losing him half a million dollars. I had to convince him that no one alive could teach his son to shoot. In some tactful way, I had to tell him that when he got drunk in the future not to make bets. I didn't know how he would take it, but it had to be said.

A half a million dollars was a hell of a lot of money to lose, but Savanto had made the bet. If he turned rough, I too could turn rough. I was being straight with him. He was getting his money back. I would even return the five hundred dollars he had advanced. To be rid of Timoteo I would be ready to give for free those days I had had him in my hair.

We were approaching Paradise City. I was expecting Raimundo to keep straight ahead, but he abruptly slowed the car, then swung on to a secondary road that led towards the sea.

'Do you know where you're going?' I asked sharply. 'The Imperial Hotel isn't this way.'

Raimundo kept on driving.

'He's moved,' was all he said.

We turned up a narrow road, hedged by sand banks. A little later, we turned on to a narrower road and he had to cut speed. After a mile or so, we came on a small, white painted house with a sandy garden full of weeds and clumps of coarse grass, and a wide, walk-around verandah. Away from the house were two sheds that served as garages.

He stopped the car at the gate, cut the engine and put the key in his pocket. He got out.

I followed him up the path. As he got half way to the house, Savanto came out through the front door. He still wore the black suit and slouch hat, and he still looked like a vulture.

He lifted his small fat hand in greeting as Raimundo stood aside and I continued on up the three steps that brought me on to the verandah.

'Come and sit down, Mr. Benson,' Savanto said. 'I was coming to see you tomorrow.' His little black eyes ran over my face and then he walked heavily to a bamboo chair and sat down, waving me to another chair. 'What have you to tell me?'

I sat down.

Raimundo climbed the steps and walked into the house. I heard him greet someone. I heard a deep male voice return his greeting.

'Well, Mr. Benson?' Savanto asked.

I took from my hip pocket the twenty-five thousand dollar bond, carefully unfolded it and offered it to him.

'This isn't the age of miracles, Mr. Savanto,' I said. 'I am sorry. It didn't work out. I also owe you five hundred dollars.'

He studied me, his face expressionless, then he took the bond, looked at it, folded it back into its creases, took out a well-worn wallet, inserted the bond and returned the wallet to his pocket.

'Do you want more money, Mr. Benson?' he asked. 'Would you be more interested if I offered a hundred thousand dollars?'

I stared at him, my heart beginning to thump. A hundred thousand dollars! I could see by the look in his eyes he was serious. It made sense. He would still be saving himself four hundred thousand. Just for a second or two I was tempted, then I thought of Lucy and the dismay that would come into her eyes if I returned to tell her the shooting was on again. Then I thought of Timoteo. I knew no money on earth would make that goon a marksman.

'No, I don't want more money,' I said. 'I couldn't earn it. No one can teach your son to shoot. There's something stopping him: a mental block. Maybe if you took him to a head shrinker, it might fix him, but I can't.'

Savanto nodded. He stared out across the neglected garden, his eyes sleepy, his small fat hands resting on his knees.

There was a long, uneasy silence.

'I'm sorry,' I said finally. 'I'll let you have my cheque for five hundred dollars. The food and drink are more or less intact. Your men can take away what's left.' I got to my feet. 'I'm sorry about the bet, but you shouldn't have made it.'

He looked up at me.

'There was no bet, Mr. Benson ... just a harmless piece of fiction. Don't go away. I want to talk to you. Please sit down.'

I hesitated. Then I remembered Raimundo had the key of my car. I remembered there was another man in the house. The instinct I have for danger was alive.

I sat down.

'Would you like a drink, Mr. Benson?'

'No, thanks.'

'Change your mind ... I am going to have one.' He looked over his shoulder and called 'Carlo!'

A giant of a man appeared in the doorway. He must have been standing just out of sight all the time Savanto had been talking to me. He was built like a boxer with enormous shoulders, a slim waist and long tapering legs. His moon-shaped face was flat and brutish, his eyes small, his nose spread across his face and he was as bald as an egg.

'Two whiskies, Carlo,' Savanto said.

The giant nodded and went away.

'That is Carlo,' Savanto said. 'He is a dangerous man when I need a dangerous man.'

I didn't say anything. I was now certain I had walked into trouble. I thought I could take on Raimundo, but not Raimundo and Carlo together.

We sat there in the shade, looking at the neglected garden and listening to the sound of the distant surf until Carlo returned, carrying a tray on which stood two glasses of whisky and ice. He put the tray down on the table and went away.

'Mr. Benson, you spoke of my son having a mental block,' Savanto said. 'You are right. He does have that. For you to understand why, I am going to tell you a little story that I hope you will find interesting.' He took one of the glasses, saluted me and sipped the whisky. 'My father lived in Venezuela: he was born there and he died there. He was a peasant and poor in spirit. He was also a dreamer and very religious. He believed a life of abject poverty was the will of God. He had two sons: myself and my brother, Antonio. My mother died of starvation. My brother and I decided to leave the hut that my father proudly called our home. This was a serious decision because the sons in this district always did what their fathers wished and my father didn't wish us to leave.' He paused, looking at me. 'There is a strong tradition among the people I come from that children have to obey their parents: it amounts to superstition. If they disobeyed their parents they came to no good. Anyway, my brother and I left this miserable hut. We came to some good. We discovered a gold mine on our travels. By that time my father had also died of starvation. My brother and I became very rich. We married: each of us had a son. My brother had Diaz. I had Timoteo. Diaz took after his father. Timoteo took after his grandfather.' Savanto shrugged. 'I became interested in politics. I was forever remembering that my mother and my father had died of starvation. My brother became interested in power. We disagreed, quarrelled and parted. Now my brother is the Chief of the Red Dragon organisation which works with the Mafia. I am the Chief of the Little Brothers who represent the rights of the peasants.' He paused to sip his whisky. 'Am I boring you, Mr. Benson?'

'No, but I don't see why you are telling me all this.'

'Be patient. You have seen something of Timoteo. He isn't an impressive man, but nor was my father. He is a dreamer and an idealist and he is intelligent. He is also sentimental. He met a girl and fell in love with her. He came to me and said he wanted to marry this girl. He brought her to me.' Savanto fumbled in his pocket. 'Have you a cigarette, Mr. Benson, you can spare? I never seem to carry cigarettes with me.'

I put my pack of cigarettes on the table. He helped himself and I gave him a light.

'As soon as I saw this girl I knew Timoteo was making a mistake. She was not for him. She was pretty and so on, but light-minded. I told him so, but he was in love.' Savanto shrugged his shoulders. 'I persuaded him to wait a year.' He studied the end of his cigarette and then went on. 'Now we come to my nephew, Diaz Savanto. He is as like Timoteo as a tiger is like a lamb. He is a big, fine-looking man; very athletic, a splendid polo player, a good shot and a great success with women. He too met this girl Timoteo had fallen in love with. He knew Timoteo was in love with her.' Savanto paused again, frowning. 'My brother and I quarrelled bitterly. Diaz despised the Little Brothers, despised me and despised Timoteo. He is a bad man, Mr. Benson. He decided this girl gave him the opportunity he had been waiting for to show his contempt for me, my son and my organisation. He kidnapped the girl, raped her and branded her. In the old days, members of the Red Dragon organisation branded their cattle with their symbol.' Savanto looked down at his fat hands, frowning. He remained like that for some moments, then went on. 'He branded this girl with the Red Dragon symbol. An insult like that can only be wiped out by death. I am the Chief of the Little Brothers. I had only to raise my hand and my nephew would die. But I am unable to do this because what he has done is a personal insult to my son. It is my son who has personally to avenge the insult.'

I moved uneasily, but I was listening.

'All the members of the Little Brothers know of this insult,' Savanto went on. 'They are waiting to hear that Diaz Savanto is dead, killed by my son's hand. They know Timoteo is taking shooting lessons. They are patient people, but they are waiting and they are becoming less patient. Diaz knows Timoteo is incapable of killing anyone. He knows Timoteo takes after his grandfather: a life is sacred and belongs to God. That was what my father thought and that is what Timoteo thinks. This is the mental block you speak of. But revenge is part of our tradition. My people don't think the way Timoteo thinks. If he doesn't kill Diaz the name of Savanto will be disgraced. I will no longer be Chief.' He finished his whisky. 'Now, Mr. Benson, perhaps you understand my problem.'

'I don't know why you are telling me this. I have returned your money and that lets me out,' I said as I got to my feet. 'I don't want to hear any more.'

He put his hand gently on my arm.

'Have patience with me for a few more minutes.' Then raising his voice, he called, 'Raimundo!'

Raimundo came out on to the verandah carrying a curious-looking instrument. It was made of iron, set in a wooden handle: the end of the iron was red hot.

'Demonstrate to Mr. Benson the Red Dragon branding-iron,' Savanto said quietly.

Raimundo pressed the red-hot iron against one of the wooden uprights of the verandah. I watched the wisp of smoke spiral away from the wood. Raimundo removed the iron, then with a quick look at me, he went back into the house.

'Please look at what he has done,' Savanto said. 'It is the brand of the Red Dragon. It is of historic interest.'

I moved over and looked at the brand-mark. It was about an inch long, depicting a crude animal with a forked tail and a snout like crocodile.

'That was branded on the face of the girl Timoteo wished to marry,' Savanto said.

I turned.

'Are you and your tribe so primitive that you can't turn this over to the police?' I said.

'Yes. It is a personal thing.'

'Did the girl think so?'

Savanto shrugged his shoulders.

'It is not the girl. It is the insult.'

'What happened to her?'

'Mr. Benson, don't become too curious. Please sit down.'

'I don't want to hear any more.'

'You are involved in this.' He stared at me. 'Let me finish. Please sit down.'

So I sat down.

'You will understand from what I have told you, I had a problem. I suspected Timoteo couldn't do what was expected of him. I heard about you: a first-class shot: a man who spent three years in the jungle as a sniper. A sniper is a legalised killer, Mr.

Benson. I decided you were the man I was looking for. I let it be known that Timoteo was taking shooting lessons. The news pleased my people and it amused Diaz because Diaz is no fool. He knew, as I suspected, that no one could teach Timoteo to shoot, but my people don't know and that is important.'

'They'll know now,' I said.

'Not if my thinking is correct,' Savanto said. 'You see, Mr. Benson, you are going to deputise for my son: you are going to kill Diaz Savanto.'

I sat for a long moment staring at him. I felt a cold prickle run up my spine.

'Your thinking is not correct,' I said.

'Mr. Benson, this is important to me, to Timoteo and to my organisation. It is not that I mind losing the power I have. I am getting old. If there was someone to replace me, then I would go, but there is no one. I represent the rights and interests of a quarter of a million peasants. Because of my efforts, they are no longer starving, but there is still much to be done. I . . .'

'Your thinking is not correct,' I repeated.

'I am now offering you two hundred thousand dollars to take my son's place. Think carefully, Mr. Benson. How many men have you already killed in cold blood? Eighty-two? What is one more life to you?'

'I was a soldier . . . a soldier has to kill. I'm no longer a soldier so I am not doing it. And let me tell you something: your son's thinking is right. If you are too primitive to know this, then take it from me.'

I got up and walked into the lobby of the house.

Raimundo was leaning against the wall close to an open door through which I could see Carlo, sitting at a table, picking his teeth with a splinter of wood.

'I want the key of my car,' I said to Raimundo.

I was set to hit him. I knew I hadn't much of a chance.

He looked at me thoughtfully, then he took the key from his pocket and tossed it to me.

I backed away, turned and started to cross the verandah.

'So you are leaving, Mr. Benson,' Savanto said.

I ignored him, going down the steps to the car.

'If you are returning to your wife, Mr. Benson, there is no need to hurry. She won't be there.'

His words came clearly to me as I was opening the door of the car. I stood for a moment feeling the hot sun on my face, then I closed the car door and came back on to the verandah.

Chapter Five

Savanto looked up at me as I came towards him. His fat, pock-marked face was expressionless; his stubby fingers stroked his moustache.

Raimundo and Carlo had come out onto the verandah. Raimundo leaned against the door-post. Carlo stood away from him, still picking his teeth with the splinter of wood.

'I'm sorry, Mr. Benson,' Savanto said, 'but I must consider the lives of a quarter of a million people ... peasants like my father: all struggling to live.'

'You can cut out the crap!' I said. 'What do you mean ... she won't be there?'

Raimundo pushed himself away from the door-post, his hands hanging loosely, and he edged towards me.

'Your wife is now under my protection. She is quite safe. Please don't be anxious, Mr. Benson.'

For a long moment I looked into the flat snake's eyes. There was sadness on the fat face, but no mercy in the glittering eyes.

'You've kidnapped her?' I asked, holding on to myself because I knew, at this moment, control was essential.

'I would prefer to say she has been taken as a hostage.'

Well, I had been warned. Raimundo had told me if I flopped I would be in trouble. I had thought this was an empty threat. Now, I knew differently. I fought down the urge to smash this elderly thug, to turn on Raimundo, to hammer my fists into Carlo's brutish face.

'Kidnapping carries a long stretch in jail, Savanto,' I said. 'Where is she?'

He continued to look at me, then he nodded approvingly.

'Sit down, Mr. Benson,' he said. 'I admire the way you are taking this. I expected trouble. If someone had kidnapped my wife, I wouldn't have been able to control myself. I would have done something foolish, but then I am a Latin-American. My blood boils too easily. But you have been a soldier and you have discipline. You know violence will achieve nothing. You tell yourself if you remain calm and listen to what I have to say, you will be able to make a good decision. So sit down, Mr. Benson, and listen to my proposal. After I have made it, you will then be able to decide what to do. You will have two alternatives: either to do what I ask or to try to outwit me. You have the freedom of choice, but I hold the trump card ... your wife. For the time being, you need not worry about her. Already, there is a woman with her. Her new home is much better than the home you provided for her. She will have everything she wants, except, of course, her freedom. I have spared no expense to make her comfortable. Please don't worry about her.'

I thought of Lucy, alone and frightened, as I walked over to the chair and sat down.

'Go ahead,' I said. 'I'm listening.'

Savanto looked at Raimundo and then beyond him at Carlo. He lifted his fat hand in a wave of dismissal. The two men went back into the house.

'Mr. Benson, because you are an expert, I have chosen you to execute Diaz,' Savanto said. 'The execution has to be arranged in such a way that my organisation and the Red Dragon organisation will believe that it was my son who fired the shot. Because you are an experienced killer I propose to leave it to you to work out how this is to be done. You have five days. Raimundo and Carlo are at your disposal. They are reliable men. Money is no object. Spend what you please to make the operation successful. When Diaz Savanto is dead, I will pay you two hundred thousand dollars.'

For a long moment I sat thinking.

'Let's look at the other side of this blackmail coin,' I said. 'Suppose I tell you to go to hell?'

He shook his head.

'You won't, Mr. Benson. I am sure of this because I am a judge of men. I know you are in love with your wife.'

'I want to hear from you what will happen to her if I don't play.'

He grimaced, then shrugged.

'I come from a primitive tribe of people.' He had now lost his sad look. He sat forward, staring at me as I was staring at him. His snake's eyes had become deadly. 'Look at that symbol ... the symbol of the Red Dragon.' He pointed to the wooden upright supporting the verandah. 'I'll send her back to you, Mr. Benson, but she will have that brand on her face if you fail me.'

He had talked of discipline. It needed all the discipline the Army had hammered into me to stop me smashing my fist in his fat, pock-marked face.

I reached for the pack of cigarettes I had left on the table, shook out a cigarette and lit it. I stared across the garden full of weeds at the distant sea.

Savanto watched me and waited.

I let him wait. Finally, I flicked the half-smoked cigarette into the garden.

'So you're the Chief of the Little Brothers who looks after a quarter of a million peasants,' I said. 'You claim to be the father of these people. You claim, because you are getting old, you don't want to keep your hold on them, but you have to because you can't find a man as good as you to take your place. So you turn blackmailer, you protect a weakling son who doesn't want to be protected and you kidnap a girl who has done no harm to anyone and if you don't get your own, murderous way, you will brand her with the symbol of the organisation you are supposed to be fighting. I wonder what your peasants would think of you if they found out the kind of animal you really are?'

The fat, pock-marked face remained expressionless.

'Go on talking, Mr. Benson. It is always good to get the bile out of one's system.'

I knew then that nothing I could say would make any difference. I had guessed this as soon as I had returned to the verandah, but I had to make a try. I was wasting time.

'Okay,' I said, 'I'll kill him for you, but I'm not taking your money. I walked into this because I thought money was all important. It is important, but not your kind of money. I'll kill him because I want my wife back.'

Savanto stroked his moustache.

'Any kind of money is important, Mr. Benson,' he said. 'Don't make a hasty decision about the money. Two hundred thousand dollars would change your way of life.' He levered himself to his feet. 'The money will be waiting for you.'

From one of the sheds away from the house the black Cadillac appeared with the chimp-faced driver at the wheel.

'I must go now, Mr. Benson.' He looked directly at me. 'I can leave this business safely in your hands?'

I returned his look, hating him.

'Yes.'

'Good. I promise your wife will remain safe. Do what I ask and she will return to you unharmed. You can rely on Raimundo. He will help you. He is as anxious as I am that this business is successfully concluded.'

He walked heavily down the steps to the car. He got in and settled himself, then the car drove away down the narrow road. Behind it, like a ghost, followed a spiral of dust.

As I watched the car disappear, Raimundo came out and

walking around me, sat down in the chair Savanto had vacated.

He made to take a cigarette from my pack, then paused.

'Mind if I use one of these?'

I was pretty near flash point, but I held on to myself.

'Use your own goddam cigarettes!' I snarled. 'Don't use mine!'

He got up, went into the house and after a moment or so, came back, smoking. He sat down again, putting a pack of Camels near my pack.

We sat there for a long uneasy minute, then he tossed the cigarette over the verandah rail.

'Feel like a fight, soldier?' he asked.

'What's that mean?'

He got up and walked down the steps into the overgrown garden. He turned, his hands resting on his hips.

'Come on, soldier ... let's fight.'

I wanted this. I wanted to smash a human face. Lucy was in the front of my mind ... alone and frightened. I wanted to smash my way out of the trap I had walked into. I wanted to beat and be beaten.

I got to my feet and started down the steps. Raimundo backed away and began to strip off his shirt. I pulled off my shirt and let it drop, then I started towards him.

He was fast as I knew he would be. I got a clip on the side of my head as I came in which warned me he could punch. I jabbed him, but his head wasn't there and I collected a solid bang in the teeth that sent me off balance. He was fast all right and moving around me, bouncing, on balance, able to shoot fast with either hand. I took two more of his punches: one split the skin under my right eye; the other made a graze on my cheek bone, then I nailed him with my right. It had all my weight and hate behind it. It exploded on his jaw and as he started to fall, I saw his eyes roll back. He went down, his head thudding on the sand.

I stood over him, my right fist aching and I waited.

After a moment or so, he opened his eyes, blinked up at me, then with a rueful grin, he got himself to his feet, but his legs were rubbery and he was staggering as he raised his fists.

The punch I had caught him with had taken most of the bile out of me.

'Let's cut it out,' I said. 'Okay?'

'If you want to go on ... come on!' He took a step forward, then sagged down on his knees. He peered at me, shaking his head to clear it. 'Have you let off enough steam, soldier?'

I caught hold of his arm and hoisted him to his feet. I helped him up the steps on to the verandah and steered him to one of the chairs. He collapsed into it, holding the side of his face. Blood was dripping from the cut under my eye. I sat down, holding my handkerchief against the cut.

We sat there like a couple of dummies for quite a while, then I removed the handkerchief. The cut wasn't bleeding any more. I picked up my pack of cigarettes and offered it to him.

He looked at me, grimaced, then took a cigarette. We lit up.

'If you have to hate someone,' he said, 'I'd rather you hate Carlo than me.'

Carlo came out on to the verandah. There was a bovine grin on his brutish face. He put two whiskies and ice on the table.

'That was a fine punch, Mr. Benson. You want to punch me too?'

I looked at him, then at Raimundo.

'Go ahead,' Raimundo said. 'Hit him. He likes it ... I don't. Listen, soldier, we have a job to do, but we can't do it if you're still full of steam. So go ahead and hit him if it'll help.'

I looked at the distant sea. *I hold the trump card ... your wife,* Savanto had said. I looked at the crude brand on the upright supporting the roof of the verandah. I thought of Lucy. This wasn't the time to thrash around like an animal caught in a net. This was something I had to handle if I wanted Lucy back, safe and unmarked.

'I take it, Savanto has some sort of plan and I have to put a polish on it. Right?' I said.

'More or less.'

'What's the plan?'

'Diaz arrives at the Paradise City airport at 22.15 on September 27th. He will be travelling with four bodyguards. There will be a car at the airport to meet him. He and his bodyguards will drive along Highway 1. I have a marked map of the route. He will arrive at the Willington estate around 23.20. I have a map of the house and grounds. He will stay there for three days. Then he drives back to the airport and takes off. Mr. Savanto wants him knocked off here ... not on his home ground: that would make too much of an uproar. So we have three days and two nights to nail him.'

'The Willington estate ... what's that?'

'It's where his new girl friend lives,' Raimundo told me. 'Nancy Willington. You've heard of her, haven't you?'

'You mean Edward Willington's wife?'

'That's the one.'

Edward Willington was the President of National Computers. He was always in the news. There were constant press photos of him shaking hands with the President, boarding his enormous yacht, getting into his Rolls and so on and so on. I remembered him as a tall, fat man around sixty-five years of age with a politician's smile and financier's eyes. He had been married three times and had married yet again a year or so ago to an eighteen-year-old model. The marriage had caused quite a newspaper yak. I hadn't paid much attention at the time, but the yak had been enough for me to remember.

'Are you telling me Willington's wife is Diaz's new girl friend?'

'That's it. They met when Willington took her with him on a business trip to Caracas. While he was making money, Diaz was taking Nancy around. Now Willington is going to Paris from September 26th to 30th. The big house is shut up. Nancy is supposed to be at the Spanish hotel until Willington comes back. There's a bungalow used for guests on the estate. That's where she is meeting Diaz.'

'How do you know all this?'

Raimundo grinned.

'We got at Nancy's coloured maid. She will be there to cook and clean while Diaz is screwing Nancy. Nancy told her the whole programme and she relayed it to me.'

'Let me look at the map of the estate.'

'Don't waste your time. I've been to the place and checked it. There would be no problem if he was on his own, but he isn't. His four boys are good. I don't say they are better shots than you, but they are good. They will be patrolling all the time.'

While he was talking, Carlo came out with a plate of sandwiches. 'Eat something, soldier,' Raimundo went on. 'You don't have to worry about her.' He was smart enough to read my thoughts. The sight of those sandwiches had turned my mind to Lucy who had been getting my lunch ready when I had left her. 'When Mr. Savanto says someone is okay, you can believe it.'

'I want to talk to her on the telephone. You make the connection and let me talk to her.'

He hesitated.

'I've got to talk to her,' I urged. 'Maybe she is safe, but she doesn't know it. If Savanto wants the job done well, I've got to talk to her.'

He chewed his sandwich while he thought, then he nodded.

'Makes sense to me. Just don't tell Mr. Savanto.'

He went into the house. I waited, my heart thumping. It was a five minute wait. To me it seemed like an hour, then he came to the door.

'She's on the line.'

I went into the hot sitting-room and picked up the telephone receiver.

'Lucy?'

'Oh, Jay . . .'

The sound of her voice, scared and unsteady, hit me under the heart.

'Are you all right?'

'Yes. Jay, what does all this mean?'

'Don't worry about it. Are you being looked after?'

'Oh, yes, but Jay! I must know . . . what's happening?'

'Don't worry. Trust me. I'll be with you in a few days. Just trust me . . .' I heard a click on the line and it went dead.

Well, I had got some kind of message over. At least, she had told me she was all right. Of course she was scared, but now I hoped she would hang on, remembering what I had said.

'Got that off your chest, soldier?' Raimundo asked. He was standing in the doorway, watching me.

I replaced the receiver.

'It helped.'

I returned to the verandah and sat down. I was now more relaxed and hungry. As Raimundo sat by my side, we both reached for sandwiches.

'If I can't nail him on the estate where do I nail him?' I asked.

'In around ten minutes you'll see.' He chewed for a moment, then went on, 'The Little Brothers are sending a witness who has to be convinced Timoteo did the shooting.'

'Who will that be?'

Raimundo spat over the verandah rail.

'Fernando Lopez. He is a big shot in the organisation and he hates Savanto. He's sure Timoteo hasn't the guts to knock Diaz off. It'll be your business to convince him.'

I didn't like the sound of this.

'If he's going to stand over Timoteo while he shoots we can give up right now.'

'Mr. Savanto will be here. He won't let him stand over him. This is something we have to work out.'

I looked at him.

'Just why are you getting involved in this? You're making yourself an accessory to murder.'

Raimundo fingered his jaw tenderly.

'I don't see it that way. Mr. Savanto did me a lot of good when I was a kid. I owe him plenty.' His black eyes hardened. 'This has got to work, soldier.'

'So he tells me or my wife gets branded.'

'When it's done you'll be a rich man. Savanto keeps his promises. You'll only have yourself to blame if he puts the iron on her.'

I felt a cold chill crawl up my spine.

'He will do it?'

'He'll do it.'

He looked at his watch, then got to his feet and went into the house. He returned, carrying two pairs of 9 x 35 binoculars. He gave me one pair, then sat down, holding the other pair on his knees. 'The bay ahead of you is part of Willington's private beach.' Again he looked at his watch. 'Take a look at the bay through the glasses and imagine you are going to shoot.'

As I picked up the glasses I heard the distant throb of a high-powered engine. I was focusing the glasses as I picked up a sleek motorboat as it came around the arm of the bay. I adjusted centre screw. The glasses were good. I now had the boat in focus. There was a fat negress wearing a white overall at the wheel. I saw the tow rope white against the blue of the sea and I shifted the glasses to the left.

The girl on the skis was completely naked. Her slim, perfectly-built body was golden brown: her straw-coloured hair streamed out behind her. I moved the centre screw a little and she came sharply into focus. I could see her dark nipples and her taut arm muscles. She looked like a sea nymph as she skimmed over the water to the far end of the bay. There was an excited, laughing expression on her young face. The boat made a sharp turn. She jumped the tow rope with the ease and confidence of an expert, then she lifted a leg and skimmed along on one ski.

She cavorted for some fifteen minutes: beautiful, exciting, sexy and thoroughly expert. Then the boat took her out of sight behind the row of palm trees that fringed the bay. I heard the motor splutter, then die.

'That's her,' Raimundo said, putting down his glasses. 'Every day at this time she skis. Diaz is one of the top skiers in South

America. It's a safe bet when he has screwed her enough, they will come out on that bay and show each other how good they are. Can you nail him from here?'

I thought about this. The target would be moving fast and constantly changing direction. I thought of the 600mm. telescopic sight which would cut down the distance to maybe a hundred feet. It wouldn't be an impossible shot, but a tricky one. Then I thought what it would mean if I missed. I looked again at the Red Dragon brand on the verandah upright. I remembered the time when I had been high in a tree with a rifle equipped with a 300mm. sight. I had waited three long, hot hours for a sniper to show: a sniper who had done a lot of damage. My arms had become stiff and my eyes, in the glare, unreliable before he raised his head into sight. The range had been close on five hundred yards. I had a split second to kill him, but I had killed him. That was three years ago. My reflexes were that much slower, but I would have Diaz in my sights for half a mile. I would be shooting with a silencer. I would have at least six shots at him without him knowing he was being shot at.

'It's a seventy-five-twenty-five chance on,' I said. 'Will she perform tomorrow?'

'Every day at this time.'

'I'll know for sure when I've looked at her through the telescopic sight.' I stood up. 'I'm going back to get Timoteo's rifle.'

Raimundo squinted up at me.

'You want me to come with you, soldier?'

'I won't run away.'

He nodded.

'Go ahead.'

It took me a little over thirty-five minutes to get back to the place I called my home. During the drive I thought of Lucy. I thought of the first night we had spent together. Unlike most girls these days she had been a virgin. I remembered her little gasp of pain as I had entered her and I remembered her gentle hands holding my head. I remembered the next three months when she had always been dithering but encouraging. I remembered her saying: *I am a little scared of you. I do see you have to be tough and hard if you are to succeed, but please try not to be tough and hard with me.*

To get her back I had to kill a man. But who was Diaz Savanto? He had shown himself to be an animal. He had raped and branded a girl who was probably as harmless as Lucy.

As I drove up the sandy road that led to the shooting school, I saw the gates were open. As I neared the bungalow I saw the red and blue Buick convertible that belonged to Detective Tom Lepski of Paradise City's police headquarters.

*

I slid out of the car, my heart thumping and I looked around. There was no sign of Lepski. I walked to the bungalow. The front door stood open. I entered the sitting-room. The table was laid for a meal. I went into the kitchen. On the stove was a frying pan with slices of ham, a saucepan of peas and another saucepan of water with a cup of rice near by. I walked into our bedroom. It was as I had left it. I looked into Lucy's closet. Her clothes were there. Nothing seemed missing.

I had a feeling of utter loneliness. This was the first time I had come home and not found her waiting for me.

I left the bungalow and headed for the shooting gallery. I had an idea I would find Lepski there. I was right. As I approached, he appeared in the doorway of the lean-to.

His cold quizzing eyes met mine.

'Hi! I was going to put in an alarm about you.'

I forced myself to meet the probing stare.

'Alarm? What do you mean?'

'I found this place deserted. I thought something was wrong.'

'Nothing's wrong. What brings you here, Mr. Lepski?'

'I was passing. I promised Mrs. Benson a recipe for a chutney my old lady used to make. Where is she?'

I was sure he had been in the house, had seen the preparations for the meal and had sniffed around as only a trained cop can sniff around.

'I've just seen her off. A friend of hers is ill. We had a panic call.'

'That's tough.' He shook his head. 'When I got here and looked around it was like another Marie Cèleste.'

'Another . . . who?'

He looked a little smug.

'The ship that was found deserted: meals on the table . . . no one aboard. I'm a *Reader's Digest* subscriber. They tell you stuff like that. When I got here, found the front door open, the table laid for a meal, the meal on the stove, no sign of life . . . it got me bothered.'

'Yeah, we had this panic call. We dropped everything and ran.'

'A friend of your wife's?'

'That's right.'

He eyed me.

'Who won?'

I gaped at him.

'Come again.'

'What was the fight about?'

I had forgotten my bruises and the cut under my eye.

'Oh, nothing. I got into an argument. I guess I flip my lid from time to time.'

'Some argument.' He rubbed the back of his neck and looked away from me. 'Your telephone isn't working.' His eyes swivelled back to me.

'It isn't?' I began to fumble for a cigarette, then changed my mind. That sort of move tells a cop he's making you nervous. 'One minute it works, the next it doesn't. You know how it is when you're as far out as we are.'

'The line's been cut.'

The back of my throat was turning dry.

'Cut? I don't understand that.'

'It's been cut.'

'Some kid ... Kids around here are hell. I'll get it fixed. I had no idea.'

'Do you usually walk out of your home leaving the front door open?'

I was getting fazed with these questions. I decided it was time to stop him.

'If it doesn't worry me, why should it worry you?'

Lepski's face hardened. He became all cop.

'Folk who are that careless make a lot of work for the police. I'm asking you: do you usually walk out of your house and leave the door open?'

'I guess so. We're miles from anyone. We often sleep with the door open.'

He regarded me, his eyes bleak.

'And the kids around here are hell?'

I didn't say anything.

'When I got here and found no one,' he went on after a long pause, 'I looked around. Did Mrs. Benson take her things with her? I looked in the closets ... that's routine, Mr. Benson. Seemed to me nothing is missing.'

'I appreciate your interest,' I said, 'but you don't have to worry. This was a panic call. We didn't have much time. My wife took all she wanted for a few days.'

He stroked his nose while he continued to look at me.

'Why isn't your pupil shooting?'

The sudden shift of ground had me fazed.

'Pupil?'

'The rich guy you are teaching who is taking up all your time.'

'Oh ... him.' My mind worked quickly. 'He quit yesterday.'

'Is that right? What was his trouble? Another sick friend?'

'No trouble. He just got bored.'

'Is that Weston & Lees rifle in the gun rack his?'

'Yes.' I was beginning to sweat and this annoyed me. 'I'm sending it back to him.'

'Why didn't he take it with him?'

I had to stop this.

'Do you care, Mr. Lepski?'

He grinned.

'I guess not.' The grin went away. 'This six hundred milimetre sight and silencer. ... Who is he planning to assassinate? The President?'

I had left the sight and silencer in the box. He must have been hunting around in earnest to have found them.

Somehow I forced a laugh.

'He's gadget-minded. You know these guys with more money than sense. Every gun gadget he sees he has to have.'

'Yeah.' Lepski nodded. 'So now you have free time? No pupil ... no wife. I've got free time tomorrow. How about me coming out here for a lesson?'

That was the last thing I wanted.

'Sorry, but I plan to join my wife. I'm shutting the school for a few days.'

'I don't seem to have any luck. Okay, we have a date on the 29th. Right?'

'That's it. I haven't forgotten.'

He thought for a moment, then said. 'That's a nice gun ... the best. I'd like to own a gun like that.'

'Me too.'

His expression turned blank as he thought. I watched him, sure when he looked like that he was dangerous.

'You mean he gave up taking lessons even when he had the telescopic sight?'

'He got bored.'

Lepski scratched the side of his face.

'Isn't money a wonderful thing? I'd like to be bored.' He took off his straw hat and fanned himself with it. 'It's goddam hot, isn't it?' Before I could agree that it was hot, he went on, 'So you're joining your wife. Where is she?' This was shot at me, quick and hard like a boxer's jab.

By now, I was very alert.

'Not all that far. Well, Mr. Lepski, I have things to do. See you on the 29th.'

'Sure. You have things to do.' He hesitated, then he turned on his cop stare. 'Keep your house locked in the future. We're not looking for unnecessary work.'

'I'll remember.'

'Well, so long, Mr. Benson. See you later.'

We shook hands, then he walked off to his car. I stood in the sun, watching until he had driven out of sight. I went back to the bungalow and cleared up. I packed a bag with enough things to last me a week. Then I found a sheet of paper and in block letters I wrote:

THE SCHOOL OF SHOOTING IS CLOSED UNTIL SEPTEMBER 28th.

I put my bag in the car, went over to the shooting gallery, locked my guns away and collected the Weston & Lees rifle, the sight and the silencer.

I drove down to the double gates, closed them and fixed the notice on the wooden upright, then I drove back to the little white house where I had a rendezvous in five days time with Diaz Savanto.

*

'I want to talk to Savanto,' I said.

We had just finished a scratch meal. Carlo's cooking was pretty bad and none of us had eaten much. The moon was on the rise and the night was hot. It was very quiet and peaceful with the moon, the sea and the swaying palms, but I wasn't at peace.

Raimundo regarded me.

'Anything you say, soldier. When do you want to see him?'

'Right now. Where is he?'

'At the Imperial. Do you want me to come along?'

'Yes.'

He looked surprised, but got to his feet and we went down to the Volkswagen.

For the past four hours I had been wandering around, getting the feel of the place and working on the problems that had to be solved before I could even think of the shot. I was aware that I hadn't much time. I now had the problems lined up and four real tricky ones couldn't be solved without Savanto's help. If he couldn't handle them, we were in trouble.

We found him sitting on the balcony of his hotel suite. He waved me to a chair.

'Sit down, Mr. Benson. You have something on your mind?'

I sat down while Raimundo propped himself against the balcony rail.

'Yes, you could say that.' I told him about Lepski's two visits. He listened, his eyes a little sleepy, his fingers doing a little dance on his knees.

'This cop is sharp,' I concluded. 'Because you tricked me into agreeing to kill Diaz, I have now given him false information he will probably check. Because you lied to me about your son not being allowed to touch a firearm I told him about a rich client who doesn't exist. Now I have told him about a sick girl friend of my wife who also doesn't exist. If he checks, I am in trouble.'

'Why should he check, Mr. Benson?'

I moved impatiently.

'Do I have to spell it out? When I kill Diaz Savanto there will be a police inquiry. If I am to shoot him while he is skiing, the police will find out fast enough that he was shot with a high-powered rifle. It won't take them long to work out from where the gunman was shooting. They will also work out the gunman was using a powerful telescopic sight. Then Lepski will remember the Weston & Lees and the six hundred millimetre sight and the silencer. He will then remember my rich pupil who doesn't exist and he will remember my wife rushed off to visit a sick friend who doesn't exist. So he will come to me and ask questions. He . . .'

Savanto raised his hand, stopping me.

'All this you are telling me presents no problem, Mr. Benson, because the situation won't arise. The police will not investigate.'

I stared at him.

'What makes you think that?'

'Because they won't know about the shooting. You haven't understood the situation. I have given it considerable thought. When I learned that Diaz was planning an adulterous three days with the wife of Edward Willington I saw this was the perfect opportunity. The last thing Nancy Willington will want is for the police, followed by the press, to ask her what Diaz Savanto was doing on her husband's private estate. Let us consider the situation from her point of view. The two of them are skiing.

Mysteriously, because you will be shooting with a silencer, Diaz drops. The boat stops. She finds he has been shot in the head. What does she do? Rush back and call the police? No. She will rely on the negress driving the boat to get the body out of the water. The negress will handle the situation. I assure you, Mr. Benson, we can rely on her. She is being extremely well paid. The body will be taken away by Diaz's men. The girl has plenty of money and she will be persuaded to pay them well. She would pay anything to avoid such publicity.' Savanto lifted his heavy shoulders. 'I assure you the police won't hear about this.'

'The girl might panic and call the police.'

'She won't be allowed to. The negress will handle her.'

I thought of this girl. I could see her, naked, young and excitedly happy on her skis. By squeezing the trigger of the Weston & Lees I would give her a future life of nightmares.

'What have you to tell me about the shooting, Mr. Benson? It is the shooting I am interested in.'

'If it wasn't for this witness of yours, there would scarcely be a problem,' I said. 'I'll be able to tell you tomorrow for certain if I can nail him while he is skiing. I want first to get a view of the girl through the telescopic sight. I am pretty sure it is an acceptable shot, but I want to be certain. If it is, then Timoteo is to do his act on the flat roof of the house. You and your witness will escort him up there. Then you two leave and you will wait on the verandah with binoculars. I want him up there at 14.30. With luck, Diaz and the girl will show around 15.00. There is a big tree at the back of the house offering plenty of cover. I'll be up there. When you and your witness leave the roof I'll join Timoteo. I'll do the shooting and get back into the tree. Timoteo joins you. It is up to him to convince your witness what a good shot he has been. What do you think?'

Savanto considered this for some moments, then he nodded.

'Yes ... it is a good plan.' He looked sharply at me, his black eyes glittering. 'You will kill him?'

'I think so, but I'll tell you tomorrow.'

'You had better be sure, Mr. Benson.'

The threat was there.

'I'll tell you tomorrow.'

I left him.

Raimundo followed me to the car. We drove back in silence.

The whole thing was completely unreal to me, but what was real was the Red Dragon brand on the verandah's upright.

Chapter Six

I spent the following morning constructing a thatched roof made
of palm leaves over part of the flat roof of the house. I had made
so many of these anti-sun shelters in Vietnam that it came as
second nature to me. Raimundo offered to help. I let him collect
the palm leaves, but when it came to the thatching, I did it myself.

If Timoteo and I had to be up on the roof for some hours at
least we would have shelter from the afternoon sun.

When I had finished, Raimundo regarded the shelter with an
approving nod.

'I can see you've done this before,' he said. 'Do you want to
eat?'

We went down and ate the sandwiches Carlo had ready.

I had spent the night in a small back room in the house while
Raimundo and Carlo had shared the larger room. I hadn't slept
much, but I had done a lot of thinking. I had now got over my
panic about Lucy. It was only when I had defeated the sick feeling of fear for her that I began to think constructively. I was
sure that Savanto was primitive enough to carry out his threat
to brand her if I failed him. I was sure he wasn't bluffing. Diaz
was staying at the Willington estate for three days. I was hoping
for time. Something might happen that could get both Lucy
and me off the hook, given time.

There was a telephone in the living-room. I considered the
possibility of calling the police and telling them what was about
to happen. This thought I put quickly out of my mind. I didn't
know where Lucy was, and they could fix her before the police
could find her, and I also would be in trouble if Raimundo or
Carlo woke up and caught me talking on the telephone. It was
too great a risk.

If I had to, I would go through with the killing, but only if I
was absolutely sure there was no other way to save Lucy. When
Diaz appeared on the first day, I could pretend to miss him. I
reasoned that Savanto would accept this if I plugged how
tricky the shot was going to be. That would give me another
night to think of a way out. Maybe it would be too risky to miss
Diaz on the second day, but at least I would have an extra night.

After eating the sandwiches, Raimundo and I went back on
the roof. I took the rifle with me.

It was hot up there, but the shade from the shelter I had built made it bearable.

Soon after 15.00 we heard the motorboat start up. I rested the rifle on the concrete surround of the roof and waited. The boat came into the bay, moving fast. I got the naked girl in the telescopic sight and adjusted the focus. I got her head in the centre of the cross wires. The sight brought her close to me. In one way I was relieved, in another way, sickened. I saw at once that this would be an acceptable shot. Even though she jinked and banked on her skis, there were long moments when she was steady enough for me to hit her in the head. Maybe Diaz would show off a lot more, but even if he did there would come a time when he would ski in a straight line and that's when I could nail him.

But I wasn't going to tell this to Raimundo. I followed her through the sight for another five minutes, then when the boat started on its return run, I lowered the rifle.

'What's the verdict, soldier?'

'It's going to be one hell of a shot,' I told him. 'It has to be a head shot. To be sure of killing him and not wounding him it has to be in the head. His head will be moving up and down all the time. I have to hit him in the brain. I'm sure I'll hit him, but I'm not sure I can hit him through the brain at this distance and with him moving. A brain shot like that is one hell of a shot.'

Raimundo put his hand under his shirt and began to scratch his chest. He looked worried.

'You've got to kill him. If you only knock the bastard's teeth out, there'll be hell to pay and we'll probably never get another chance to nail him.'

'You don't have to tell me. I'm beginning to think this plan isn't good enough.'

Raimundo swore softly.

'You'd better not tell Savanto that! He picked you for a first-class shot. You'd better be a first-class shot!'

'He knows nothing about shooting,' I said. 'That's an eight-hundred-yard moving target and it has to be a brain shot . . . an inch square. There are less than five men in the world who could guarantee such a shot.'

'You'd better be one of them!' His voice was worried and savage.

'Shut up! I want to think.'

He wasn't so angry as worried. He had lost his cocky confidence. I wondered if Savanto would take it out of him as well as Lucy and myself if there was a foul up.

Then out of the blue a germ of an idea dropped into my mind. I paused to light a cigarette, then I asked. 'Who owns this house?'

The question surprised him.

'What's that to do with you?'

'Is the owner likely to walk in on us?'

'Forget it! There are dozens of places like this for hire. We hired it.'

I thought that was likely, but I wanted to know for sure. *Dozens of places like this along the coast for hire.* My mind worked swiftly. If Savanto had hired this place, why not another in which to hold Lucy?

The germ of my idea began to grow. How could I find out? Then another idea dropped into my mind. So that I could think about it, I began to take the telescopic sight off the rifle. I was aware that Raimundo was watching me curiously.

'Let me see the plan of the Willington estate,' I said.

He scratched some more under his shirt.

'What's that got to do with this?'

'I want to look at it.'

'I've told you, soldier, Diaz's men will be there. Get that idea out of your head.'

'There will only be four of them.'

'That's plenty. They are professionals.'

I had to bluff him if I were to work out this idea.

'I once killed a sniper who was surrounded by more than a hundred trained troops. Four good men wouldn't worry me.'

He stared at me.

'You mean you think . . .'

'We're wasting time!' I put on my Army bark. 'Show me the plan!'

We left the room and went down to the sitting-room. He found the plan and spread it out on the table.

'Okay, take some fresh air,' I said as I sat down.

He hesitated, not liking being ordered around, then shrugging, he went out on to the balcony where Carlo was sleeping.

I spent some minutes examining the map. The Willington house stood in a couple of acres of lawns and flower beds. At the back of it was dense forest land with paths cut through it. To the right of the house was a swimming pool. Away from the house was the guest bungalow. This too had its swimming pool and was also backed by trees. The forest extended from the bungalow down to the sea where the boat house was. The other boundaries were surrounded by high walls. If I had charge of four bodyguards, I would have two men patrolling the paths by the boat house which was obviously the most vulnerable entrance. I would have the other two men patrolling around the bungalow.

I sat staring at the map while I considered the idea that had come into my mind. It was a ninety-five to five bet, but even odds as low as this must be taken.

I called Raimundo.

'You've had a look at this place?'

'Sure. I told you.'

'How about the walls?'

He made an impatient movement.

'They are fifteen feet high with an alarm cable operated by an electronic system. You have only to touch the top of any part of the walls to set off the alarm.'

'You're sure?'

'I'm sure! I set the alarm off. The two resident guards and two patrol cops arrived in less than ten minutes.'

'How about the boat house?'

'You can't take a boat in there. There's an alarm wire outside the harbour that sets off a warning.'

'Could you swim in?'

He thought, frowning and uneasy, then he shrugged.

'I guess so, but there'll be a guard there.'

'Can Timoteo swim?'

'Yes, he's good, but you're wasting time, soldier. Suppose you and Timoteo get into the estate, how about Lopez?'

I had forgotten Lopez.

'I'm looking for angles,' I hedged. 'I'm taking a look at the estate. It's just possible I might find a better way of getting at him than trying to hit him on skis.'

Raimundo became suspicious.

'You're wasting time.'

'We have time to waste. I'm going.'

He hesitated.

'I'll come with you. When are you going? Tonight?'

'I'm going right now.'

'Are you crazy? There are two guards there. We could walk into them and cook the deal.'

'You didn't tell me guards were there already.'

'They're always there. Willington has valuable stuff in the house, but when Diaz arrives, they leave. The girl has fixed it with the Security Agent. The negress told us. They come back when Diaz leaves, but they are there now.'

'Can you swim?'

He didn't know it, but to me this was the sixty-four thousand-dollar question. If he was a good swimmer, I was in trouble. My hopes rose when I saw him hesitating.

'I can manage.'

'What's that mean? Can you swim a quarter of a mile? I want to take off from here.' I pointed to the map. 'That's around a quarter of a mile to the harbour.'

'I wouldn't want to swim that far.'

'Okay, so you don't come with me.'

As I started towards the door, he caught hold of my arm. His face had turned vicious.

'No tricks, soldier! You make one mistake and your wife will get branded!'

I hit him a back-hand swipe that sent him reeling across the room. He thudded against the wall, bounced off and came at me. He was so mad he forgot to get on balance. As he rushed at me like a charging bull I hung one on his jaw. It was a block buster of a punch and he went out like a match flame in a gale.

I heard a sound behind me and I turned swiftly. Carlo stood gaping in the doorway of the french windows.

'Sweep him up and put him to bed,' I said. 'I'm going out.'

His brutish face showed bewilderment. I didn't give him a chance to begin thinking. I shouldered him aside and went down the steps and started across the sand dunes towards the distant arm of the bay.

*

It was a longer swim than I had thought but it didn't worry me. During my Army days I had swum five miles under pressure with Vietcong bullets splashing around me from time to time. I took it easy, and after a while, I came within sight of the Willington boat house. Slowly and cautiously, I swam towards it. There was a small harbour and I could see the motor boat. I swam just outside the entrance to the harbour, looking for any sign of life, but the place seemed deserted. Raimundo had said there was an alarm cable guarding the harbour. I didn't think it likely it would be operating during the day, but I wasn't taking a chance of alerting the two resident guards. I dived deeply and swam along one of the walls of the harbour entrance, then surfaced by the motor boat.

As I came up, shaking the water out of my eyes, a girl's voice called, 'Hi! Do you know you're trespassing?'

I looked up. Nancy Willington was standing on the cabin roof, looking down at me. She had on the skimpiest bikini I have ever seen: a joke of a bikini that was only just enough to cover her nipples and her crotch. At close quarters she was the most sensational-looking woman I had seen. Woman? Perhaps not yet ... not mentally a woman. She reminded me a little of Brigitte Bardot when she had first set the movie screen alight.

'I didn't know anyone was here,' I said, treading water. 'I'm sorry ... excuse me. I guess I've come to the wrong place.'

She laughed, leaning forward to look down at me, her full breasts threatening to escape from the tiny halter.

'Do you usually swim to people's places?'

'I said I was sorry, didn't I?' I started to swim, not fast but with purpose towards the harbour exit.

'Hey! Come back! I want to talk to you!'

I had gambled on her curiosity. The ninety-five to five chance looked as if it could pay off.

I turned round and swam back to the boat. I caught hold of the mooring-rope.

'I didn't mean to trespass.'

'Come aboard,' she said. 'Do you want a drink?'

I swung myself on to the boat's deck. I was wearing only a pair of white cotton trousers. They were sopping wet and they stuck to me. I could have been naked. I didn't think this would faze her, and I had too much on my mind for it to faze me.

She came off the cabin roof and joined me. Her eyes ran over me, missing nothing and she gave me a gamin grin.

'Some man!' she said.

'You think so? Okay ... some girl!'

She laughed.

'What are you doing here?'

'I am looking for my wife.'

This was the idea that had come to me while I was talking to Raimundo. I had to find Lucy. This girl knew the district. She just might know of a villa or a bungalow that had been recently rented.

'Your wife?' Her green eyes widened. 'Have you lost her?'

I couldn't tell her the truth. If I did, she would think only of herself. She would be on the telephone in a moment to warn Diaz to keep away. So I had to lie to her.

'I've lost her,' I said, 'but I'm not bothering you with this.

I'm a stranger around here. I saw this place and wondered if she was here. Sorry . . .'

'You're the craziest man I've ever met!' she exclaimed. 'You mean you are swimming along the coast, looking for your wife? I don't believe it!'

'I guess it's crazy.' I made my voice harsh. 'I haven't a boat so what else can I do? I've an idea she is somewhere along here so I'm looking.'

'You lost her? You mean she's left you?'

I gave her my hard Army look.

'Sorry I trespassed. I'll get going.'

'Don't go temperamental on me.' She cocked her head on one side and gave me a sexy look. 'I've nothing to do and God! am I *bored*! I'll help you. We can go in the boat.' She sat on the cabin roof. 'Tell me about it.'

'Why should you care? It's a personal thing. I want my wife back. There's a chance she's using a house along this coast. The rest is my business.'

She pouted.

'You don't have to shout at me. She might be happy without you. Have you thought of that?'

'What the hell has that to do with you?' I barked. 'I'm going to find her!'

She blinked. I was sure no man had ever spoken to her in that tone of voice.

'You're right out of a cave,' she said. 'If I were your wife, I would love you. I'll help. I know all the houses along this coast for around five miles.'

'He will have rented a place. Do you know the ones for rent?'

'Has she run off with some man? She must be soft in the head!'

'So she's soft in the head. When I find her I'm going to give her a hiding. She's been aching for a hiding ever since I married her and she's going to get it.'

Her eyes lit up.

'I wish someone would give me a hiding,' she said. 'I need it. I wish . . .'

'To hell with what you need.' I was now sure I was handling her right. 'I know what my wife needs and that's what she's going to get. Do you know the houses for rent along this strip?'

'Yes. There are three about half a mile from here. About two miles further on there's another . . . a good one.'

'Let's go to look at them.'

'Don't you want a drink?'

'I'll have that later.' I stared at her. 'Let's go.'

She went down into the cabin and started the engine. While I had been talking to her, I kept looking towards the forest that hid the guest bungalow from the boat house, wondering if the negress was watching me, but I didn't see her. I went down into the cabin as the girl began to reverse the boat out of the harbour.

'I'm Nancy,' she said. 'What's your name?'

'Max.' It wasn't a lie. Max is my second name.

She looked at me over her shoulder.

'I like Max. It's a gorgeous name.' She cleared the harbour. 'What do we do now, Max?'

'Take her along the coast, not too fast and not too close.'

'Aye, aye, Captain.' She giggled. 'Did you and her boy friend fight?'

I was always forgetting the marks from Raimundo's fists on my face.

'Not him . . . I got into an argument.'

'I like men who fight. What happened?'

I looked at her. Her eyes were unnaturally bright. I could see under the thin material of her bra that her nipples had come erect.

'Why should you care?'

She pouted.

'I like a good fight. I like it when two men . . .'

'Skip it! What's that house we're coming to?'

She grimaced, then looked to where I was pointing.

'It belongs to Van Hesson. He's quite a gorgeous man, but his wife is the worst kind of creep. Don't let them see you. She would tell my husband.'

We passed the house. I could see a number of people on the lawn under gay sun umbrellas.

Nancy advanced the throttle and we swept past the place.

'Some women are drags, aren't they?' She giggled. 'She's terrified her husband is going to lay me. She won't let him come near me.'

'How about this one?'

We were approaching another house built on the same lines as the previous one.

'That's rented. He's gorgeous to look at. She's building a baby. She's enormous. He doesn't leave her for a second. I've never been able even to speak to him.'

We went on, passing two more houses. Two elderly people

on the lawn of one and a party of old, fat people, playing cards under the shade of the trees at the other.

I was beginning to think the ninety-five to five chance wasn't going to pay off.

'You see the cape ahead?' Nancy said, putting her hand on my naked shoulder. 'That's the place I was telling you about. It belongs to Jack Dexter. He's marvellous, but God! his wife's a drip! Right now they are in the South of France. The place has been rented. Jack hates renting his houses – he has around six of them – but she's so mean, she insists.'

I was beginning to get worried. Time was running out.

'Are there any more rented houses along here?'

'Dozens of them, but they are all gruesome . . . strictly for the tourist trade. This one's nice.'

Graceful cypress trees screened the approach to the house. I could see a harbour, then as we got closer, a powerful motor boat. Beyond the harbour was a sandy beach.

As we came around the screen of trees, I saw an expanse of lawn and a ranch-type house surrounded by flower beds packed with multi-coloured begonias.

'That's Jack Dexter's place,' Nancy said. 'It's nice, isn't it? I haven't had time yet to find out who has taken it.'

I wasn't listening.

Sitting on the lawn under the shade of a spider orchid tree was Timoteo Savanto.

*

My immediate reaction on seeing Timoteo was to shout to Nancy to steer into the harbour, but I checked the impulse. There was a remote chance that Lucy wasn't there. I felt sure she was, but I couldn't take that chance.

'That's not the boy friend?' Nancy asked. She had joined me at the cabin window and was looking at Timoteo. 'He looks a drip, doesn't he?'

Timoteo had found another pair of sun goggles. At the sound of the motor boat, he looked towards us, the sun reflecting on the black glass of the goggles. Although I knew he couldn't see me at this distance and through the blue anti-glare glass of the cabin window, I moved back a little.

'No . . . that's not him,' I said.

I looked searchingly at the ranch house. Then I was thankful

I had checked the impulse to take the boat into the harbour. I saw Nick in his yellow-and-red shirt, standing on the verandah looking towards us. I saw two other men in white ducks and sweat shirts suddenly appear around the building. They too looked towards us.

'Hey! A house full of men!' Nancy said excitedly. 'Shall we call in and say hello?'

'No. How far is the next place?'

'About a mile.' Reluctantly she opened the throttle and the boat surged forward.

We looked at four other houses. I didn't want her to know I had found my objective. After the fourth house, I said, 'I guess this is a waste of time. It was a long chance. She's probably at a hotel or taken an apartment. We'll go back.'

'There are still dozens of places along this coast you haven't seen,' Nancy said. 'Don't be faint-hearted.'

'We'll go back.'

She shrugged and turned the boat. We returned at high speed. As we flashed by Savanto's place, I saw Timoteo was no longer in the garden. The two men in white ducks were sitting on the verandah. There was no sign of Nick.

As we neared the Willington harbour, Nancy slowed the boat.

'Come and have dinner with me. I'm all alone. We can talk about your wife,' she said.

'No, I've got to get on,' I said. 'Thanks for your help.'

She cut the engine and moved close to me.

'Don't rush off, Max. Let's have fun. There's lots of time to look for your wife.'

'Thanks for your help.' I pushed by her and gained the deck. I dived into the sea and began a fast crawl away from the boat. After a couple of hundred yards, I eased off and looked back. She was standing on the cabin roof, her hands on her hips, her legs wide apart.

'You stinker!' she shouted. 'I hope you drown!' Then she waved.

I waved back and continued on my way.

I was pretty sure the ninety-five to five chance had paid off, but I wasn't certain that Lucy was there. If I had seen her I would have borrowed Nancy's telephone and alerted the police, but that would be asking for trouble if they walked in and didn't find her.

As I swam back, I decided I would tell Raimundo that if the ski shot failed, it would be worth the risk of taking Timoteo to the Willington estate. I would show him on the map how it could be done.

I came out of the sea and started across the sand dunes. As I approached the house I saw Carlo on the verandah. I scarcely noticed him because I saw Savanto was sitting in one of the chairs, looking towards me. The sight of him, like a black vulture, made my heart skip a beat.

He stared stonily at me as I came up the steps.

'So you've been for a swim, Mr. Benson,' he said.

'That's right. I . . .' I got no further.

I was facing him, my back half turned to Carlo. I saw him move. I started to turn, but I was much too late. What felt like a steel bar which must have been the side of his hand slammed down on the back of my neck. My brain exploded in a flash of white light; there was complete darkness.

Agonising pain and the smell of scorching brought me back to consciousness. I heard myself yelling: it was a sound I didn't think possible to come from me: a sound I had once heard when one of my men had been hit in the stomach by shrapnel. I clenched my teeth and bit the scream back. I opened my eyes. Dimly, and out of focus, I saw Carlo bending over me. There was this awful pain raging in my chest. I heaved myself to my feet. A huge hand came from nowhere and slapped across my face. I felt myself falling. My back hit the top of the verandah steps and I felt myself slithering down them. I sprawled on the hot sand.

I lay there, riding the pain, my mind willing my body to get up so I could kill this brutish ape. I saw him coming down the steps and somehow I dragged myself to my feet. I swung at him. Again his hand slapped my face and again I sprawled on my back. I looked up at him, hating him. If it hadn't been for the raging pain in my chest, I would have got up again, but the pain took the guts out of me.

Then Raimundo came down the steps. He and Carlo grabbed me, dragged me upright and hustled me up the steps. They slammed me down into a chair.

Raimundo said quietly, 'You had it coming, soldier. Now take it easy. I'll fix the burn.'

I looked down at my chest. I had been branded with the Red Dragon on the right side of my chest. The pain still raged. I thought of Lucy with this brand on her face and how she would suffer. The thought shocked the vicious fury out of me. I sat there, staring at the brand, riding the pain. Raimundo came back. He dabbed on yellow anti-burn ointment. His fingers were gentle.

When he had finished, he moved away. I became aware that Savanto was watching.

'I warned you, Mr. Benson, not to try tricks. This isn't a game,' he said. 'Now, perhaps you will realise it. Now, perhaps you will realise how your wife could suffer.'

'Yes,' I said. I had myself under control. He was right. Up to this moment I had hoped he was bluffing, but now I knew this was no bluff.

'You talked to Mrs. Willington,' Savanto said. 'Did you tell her about the shooting?'

'No.'

He studied me, his black eyes glittering.

'I hope you are not lying. If Diaz doesn't come out on the bay, then I will know you have lied. I will avenge myself on your wife. Do you understand?'

'Yes.'

He nodded, his eyes still probing my face.

'There now seems doubt that you will hit him when he is ski-ing. Is that right?'

'I'll hit him, but I don't guarantee to kill him.'

The pain from the burn was subsiding. I looked down at the livid red mark on my chest. I imagined Lucy having to wear that mark on her face for the rest of her days. I suddenly didn't give a damn about Diaz Savanto.

'I told you this is the age of miracles,' Savanto said. 'I expect a miracle from you.'

I knew, after seeing Nancy in the telescopic sight, that I could kill Diaz. I would kill him and this nightmare would finish.

I looked steadily at him.

'I'll kill him,' I said.

Our eyes locked.

'Would you say that again, Mr. Benson?'

'I'll kill him.'

He nodded, then heaved himself out of the chair.

'Yes, I was sure I had chosen the right man,' he said, half to himself. 'Yes, you will kill him.' He moved to the top of the verandah steps, then he took off his hat, looked inside it, then put it back on his head. 'I expected trouble from you, Mr. Benson. You are a man of character. I am sorry I had to deal so harshly with you. I can understand you didn't realise how serious this affair is. You know now. It is better for you to suffer to find out this is a serious business than for your wife to suffer. I again assure you that she will be returned to you ... a little frightened, of course, but quite unharmed. You have said you will kill him. I am satisfied.' He looked beyond me at Raimundo. 'Give me a cigarette.'

Raimundo shook his head.

'Your Doc says you should lay off cigarettes, Mr. Savanto.'

Savanto held out his hand.

'Fortunately for me, you are not my doctor. A cigarette!'

Carlo came forward with a pack. He lit the cigarette for Savanto who continued to stare at Raimundo.

'You see? Carlo does what I ask.'

In spite of the pain from the burn, I was suddenly alert. I looked at Raimundo.

'Carlo is an animal,' he said quietly. 'I am more responsible.'

'Yes.' Savanto drew in smoke and let it drift down his nostrils. He looked at me. 'You have been clever, Mr. Benson. You wanted to find your wife. You have found her. She is there with Timoteo. Now I have your word that you will kill Diaz I am pleased to tell you this. You have seen the house. She has everything she needs. I told you that. I didn't expect you to believe me, but now you have seen for yourself. It is a very beautiful house, isn't it?'

I didn't say anything.

'She is quite well and safely guarded, Mr. Benson,' Savanto went on. 'She is very well guarded.' There was a long pause while he puffed at his cigarette, then he said, 'Tomorrow at 14.00, Timoteo will come here. At 14.30 I and Lopez will arrive. You are entirely responsible for the arrangements and the successful conclusion of the operation.' He stared at me, his black eyes like stones. 'Is that understood?'

The veil of this nightmare was smothering me.

'Yes,' I said.

*

The shadows from the palm trees were lengthening. The sun was sinking in a blood-red glow that lit up the horizon. The light turned the sand dunes into lunar formations. It was hot: a tropical evening with no wind and complete silence.

I was lying on the bed by the window in my small, airless room. In spite of the ointment the burn was still painful. To forget the pain, my mind moved into the past. I thought of my first meeting with Nick Lewis when he had told me the school was for sale. This meeting had started the nightmare. I thought again of my first meeting with Lucy and of our first wonderful month together. I thought of the black Cadillac coming up the drive and of our hopes that here at last was a good paying client. It all seemed a long time ago. I wondered what Lucy was doing at this moment. I was thankful she didn't know what was happening to me. I had told Savanto I would kill Diaz ... so I would kill him.

During my service in Vietnam I had killed eighty-two Vietcong: an average of twenty-seven hostile men a year. Most of them had been snipers like myself: a professional killing a professional. I could have been killed myself, but I had been lucky and that shade better at concealing myself and moving more silently through the jungle than they. I had dreamed of the first few snipers I had killed, but after a while I had become callous. But I knew I would have Diaz on my conscience in spite of knowing he was less than an animal, and in spite of knowing I was forced to kill him. This would be something I would have to live with for the rest of my days. It was essential to me that Lucy should never know. This killing had to be something I wasn't sharing with anyone ... especially Lucy.

I watched the sun go down and darkness settle over the sea. The moon wouldn't be up for another half hour. This was the long moment of twilight and stars that Lucy and I always liked.

Then the thought that had been nagging at the back of my mind suddenly came alive.

Would Lucy and I be safe after I had killed Diaz?

Savanto had said he was a man of his word. He had said Lucy would be returned to me unharmed. He had said he would pay me two hundred thousand dollars if I would take his son's place, but he was in the position to make promises. I touched the brand on my chest. A man who could do that, I thought, could do anything. What could be more convenient to him, after I had killed Diaz than to wipe both of us out? By wiping us out he would save himself two hundred thousand dollars and get rid of two witnesses who could testify that his son hadn't killed Diaz.

Was Lucy already dead?

The thought made me start upright.

Had he had her killed already?

The door opened and the overhead light came on, blinding me. I blinked as I turned my head.

Raimundo came into the room. He shut the door. He was carrying a glass of what looked like whisky and water.

'How does it go, soldier?' he asked, moving close to the bed.

'I'm all right. Why should you care?'

'You must have some sleep. The burn hurting?'

'What do you think?'

He looked down at my chest and grimaced.

'I've brought you some sleeping pills.' He set down the glass and a screw of paper on the bedside table. 'You must sleep. To-morrow's important.'

I thought of Diaz on skis, jinking over the waves. I knew I wouldn't sleep without pills. If I didn't sleep and get relaxed, the shot would be impossible.

I stared up at him, remembering how Savanto had looked at him, sure there had been distrust in Savanto's black, glittering eyes.

'Is she alive?' I asked.

He stiffened.

'What do you mean, soldier?' His voice went down to a whisper.

'Who's kidding who?' I too lowered my voice. 'After I have killed Diaz I have an idea my wife and I will cease to exist. Has he had her killed already?'

'Nothing like that is going to happen.' There was uneasiness in his voice and his eyes shifted from mine.

'That's what you say.'

'Listen, soldier, Savanto is a big man. He has done much good. He helps people. He is helping his son. When he gives his word, you can depend on it.'

'A man who could do this,' I looked down at the brand, 'could do anything.'

'He had to make you see sense, soldier,' Raimundo said. 'You were acting like a goon.'

'Is she still alive?' I repeated.

'Do you want to talk to her?' He wiped the sweat off his face with the back of his hand. 'I'll take a chance. It's a hell of a chance, soldier, but if it will make you happy, I'll try.'

I hesitated. It was enough for me to know he was sure that Lucy was still alive and he was being co-operative. It would be stupid to take a risk.

'No.' I paused, looking up at him. 'I'll tell you something. I don't think he trusts you any more. I think you could be in as much trouble as I am.'

'That's crazy talk!' But something I thought looked like fear jumped into his eyes. 'Now listen, soldier, you have got to fix Diaz! Make no mistake about it!' Suddenly he stiffened and looked hurriedly over his shoulder, then back to me. 'Take these pills.' His voice had become loud and harsh. 'You've got to sleep.'

The door had opened silently and I saw Carlo standing in the doorway.

I took the pills while Raimundo stood over me. When he was sure I had swallowed them, he turned round and started for the door.

Carlo, his little ape's eyes shifting, stepped back.

'You want something?' Raimundo demanded aggressively.

Carlo grinned like an idiot.

'I didn't know where you had got to.'

Raimundo snapped off the light.

'You know now.'

He went out of the room and shut the door.

I lay in the darkness for only a few minutes before the pills hit me.

Chapter Seven

'Are you awake, soldier?'

I opened my eyes. The hot sunlight coming through the half-open shutters made me blink. I lifted my head from the sweat-soaked pillow. Raimundo was standing by the bed, looking down at me.

'I'm awake.'

I made the effort and swung my feet to the floor. I felt dopey. The pills he had given me certainly had carried authority.

'What's the time?'

'Just on twelve.' He put a cup of steaming black coffee on the bedside table. 'How are you feeling?'

Although my chest was still sore, the raging pain had gone.

'I'm all right.'

'Diaz arrived late last night. He should be tired of screwing her by now. With luck, he'll come out on the bay.'

I had nothing to say. After regarding me, he left the room. I sipped the coffee and smoked. When I had finished the coffee, I stuck my head under the cold shower. I was careful not to let the water get near the burn.

By the time I had shaved, I was feeling pretty good. The sleep had relaxed me. I put on cotton slacks and a shirt. The brand looked ugly, but it wasn't inflamed. When I began to button the shirt, the touch of the cotton made me wince so I left the shirt open. I went out on to the verandah.

Raimundo was sitting there, cigarette dangling between his lips. I joined him, sitting in a chair close to his.

'Where's Carlo?' I asked.

'I've given him something to do. Forget him. How do you feel?' He looked at the brand, then at me.

'Okay.'

'Sure?'

'I'm all right,' I said impatiently.

'So is your wife, soldier.'

It was now my turn to stare at him.

'That's easy to say.'

'We ran out of whisky. I went over to the other place this morning for a refill. I saw her. She's okay.'

It was hard to believe he was lying.

'She's okay,' he repeated. 'Timoteo is Savanto's heir. He draws a lot of water.'

'What has that to do with my wife?'

He ran his fingers through his heavy black hair.

'Timoteo is looking after her. You don't have to worry.'

I remembered a conversation I had had with Lucy. It seemed a long time ago but the echoes of our voices came clearly to me:

You mean he's fallen for you. Is that it?

I suppose so. You don't mind, do you?

So long as you haven't fallen for him.

A surge of uneasiness ran through me.

'This is the day,' Raimundo went on. 'It's up to you now. By tonight, you could be a rich man, soldier. You . . .' He broke off as we saw Carlo coming across the sand.

Raimundo got to his feet.

'Sure you're feeling okay?'

'Yes.'

'It won't be long now . . . we'd better eat.'

He joined Carlo and they went into the house.

I sat still, feeling the heat of the sun as it was reflected off the white sand while I stared across the dunes to the sea.

I thought of Timoteo.

Lucy had said: *We think alike.*

She had also said: *Since this happened, you've become some-one I don't know.*

Raimundo came out on to the verandah. He put a plate of sandwiches on the table.

'Something on your mind, soldier?' he asked as he sat down.

'Do you have to ask stupid questions?'

After a long pause, he said uneasily, 'You'd better eat. It could be a long afternoon. Like some beer?'

'Why not?'

He got up and went back into the house. By the time he had returned with two glasses of beer, I had forced Timoteo out of my mind.

We drank and ate in silence. When we had finished, I got to my feet.

'I'll fix the rifle.'

'Anything I can do?'

'No.'

I cleaned and loaded the rifle, then clipped on the telescopic sight and screwed on the silencer. As I completed the operation, Raimundo came to the doorway.

'All okay, soldier?'

I suddenly realised he was much more jittery than I was. I was jittery enough but I could see he was really steamed up.

'Sure.' I moved round him, carrying the rifle and went up the stairs and up the ladder to the roof. I put the rifle by the con-crete parapet in the shade. I looked across the empty bay. Would Diaz show? The chances were that he would, but he might not. If he didn't, Savanto would imagine I had warned him. He had said: *I will avenge myself on your wife.*

Raimundo came up on the roof.

'Any problems?' he asked.

I had had about all I was going to take from him.

'For God's sake, can't you leave me alone?' I snarled at him. 'You're driving me crazy!'

'I'm driving myself crazy, soldier. I'm as responsible as you.'

'Have you only just found that out?'

I walked across the roof and looked up at the big tree with its leafy, overhanging branches. I got up on the parapet, caught hold of one of the branches and swung myself up. It was an easy climb. I had only to step from one branch to the next until I was high enough to be out of sight. But I had to be sure.

I sat astride one of the branches, my back resting against the trunk and looked down. The dense foliage hid the roof, but not the bay.

'Can you see me?' I shouted down.

I heard Raimundo walk across the roof. There was a long pause, then he said, 'I don't see a damn thing except leaves. Move a little.'

I swung my legs.

'I can hear you, but I can't see you.'

I came down slowly and cautiously: no branches swayed, no leaves rustled. When I joined Timoteo on the roof, Savanto's witness must have no suspicion that Timoteo wasn't alone.

I dropped lightly to the roof by Raimundo's side.

'You're certain you couldn't see me?'

'I didn't even hear you as you came down.'

I looked at my strap watch. In another ten minutes Timoteo would be here. I moved to the parapet to stare across the bay. Raimundo joined me.

'You said you saw my wife. What was she doing?' I asked, not looking at him.

He hesitated.

'Doing?' I could see my question had fazed him. 'She was talking to Timoteo.' He rubbed the back of his neck. 'He's a great talker. When anyone will listen to him, he talks all the time.'

We think alike.

'She didn't look . . . unhappy?'

'You don't have to worry about her, soldier. She's all right.'

'What's this about Timoteo being Savanto's heir?'

'When the old man dies, Timoteo takes over the Little Brothers.'

'Will he want to?'

Raimundo shrugged.

'That's the way the old man has fixed it. Timoteo could make a good leader. He's no fool. He's educated. It's just his bad luck to get caught in this set-up. This is something he can't handle.'

We both heard the sound of an approaching car. We moved together to the other side of the roof.

The black Cadillac with the chimp-faced driver at the wheel was coming up the road. Timoteo, wearing his big black hat and his sun goggles was sitting at the back of the car. By his side was one of the men I had seen from Nancy's boat: a powerfully built, swarthy man, wearing white ducks.

'Here he is,' Raimundo said and started towards the trap, leading down to the house.

'Send him up,' I said. 'I'll wait here.'

He nodded and slid down the ladder.

I sat on the parapet and waited. After a delay, Timoteo, hiding behind his sun goggles, came up the ladder on to the roof. Following him came the man in the white ducks. I gave him a quick look. I had run into men like him in the Army: dangerous, rebellious, shifty and very sure of himself. He stood away from me, his hands on his hips, a watchful expression on his swarthy face.

At the sight of me, Timoteo came to an abrupt halt. The black goggles were directed towards me. At least, he was looking at me.

Although it hurt, I had buttoned my shirt. I wasn't ready to show him what his father had done to me.

The sight of him set my blood moving hot through my veins. I wanted to slam my fist into his face. Into my mind came the picture of him and Lucy paddling, side by side, talking. *Since this happened you've become someone I don't know.*

'Do you want me to explain what is going to happen?' I said.

He just stood there, sweat glistening on his face.

'The idea is,' I said, speaking slowly as if talking to an idiot, 'your cousin will come on skis out there. He . . .'

'Yes, I know.' His voice was unsteady and husky.

'You know? That's fine.' I felt a spurt of vicious rage run through me. Because this thin creep was incapable of shouldering his own responsibilities, I had been blackmailed into cleaning up his mess for him. I walked slowly up to him. 'So you know?' I repeated. 'So you know I am being forced to kill a man because you haven't the guts to do it yourself. You know I am being blackmailed by your ape of a father to kill this man: a murder I will have on my conscience for the rest of my days. You know all that, do you, you goddam, gutless talker?'

The man in the white ducks suddenly came between Timoteo and myself.

'Shut your flapping mouth!' he snarled viciously.

I was now burning with rage. I swung a punch at him that carried all my hate with it. If it had caught him, it would have flattened him, but it didn't. He was very professional.

Then Raimundo arrived. He slid between me and the man in the white ducks and caught hold of my arms.

'Cool it, soldier!'

I threw off his hands and moved back.

'Set him up,' I said. 'Get him ready to look like a killer.' I moved across so I could see Timoteo who was still standing motionless. 'How do you feel, killer?' I shouted at him. 'Are you proud of yourself? It's easy to talk to my wife, isn't it, killer? I'd like her to be here to watch me kill a man who raped and branded your girl because you haven't the guts to do it yourself! I'd like her to be here!' I was now yelling at him.

Raimundo moved between us.

'Will you cool it, soldier?' he implored.

I got hold of myself.

'Okay.' I drew in a deep breath. 'Take him away. The sight of him makes me want to throw up.'

The man in the white ducks touched Timoteo's arm. Timoteo turned and moving like a zombie, went down the trap and out of sight.

I sat on the parapet in the shade while I got control of myself. Raimundo sat away from me, every now and then, looking anxiously at me.

After a while, I said, 'That creep gets me. I'm okay. Don't flip your lid. When they arrive, bring him and Lopez up here. When Lopez has had a look around, take him down to the verandah. Tell Timoteo to alert me when Lopez has gone. I can't see the roof from where I'll be. Try to make him look like a killer. The way he looks now, Lopez won't believe he could kill a fly.'

'Yeah. Are you sure you're all right?'

I stared at him.

'I'll kill him if that's what's on your mind.'

We looked at each other for a long moment, then he nodded.

'I'm sorry you walked into this, soldier,' he said. 'It doesn't do a damn bit of good, but I want you to know.'

'That's right. It doesn't do a damn bit of good.'

We sat there in silence for around twenty minutes, looking towards the road. Then Raimundo said sharply, 'They're coming.'

I had already heard the approaching car.

'Just get him to look like a killer,' I said, and climbing on to the parapet, I swung myself up into the tree. I climbed to the branch where I had sat before and sat astride it.

'Okay?' I called down.

'Yes.' There was a pause, then he said, 'Good luck, soldier.'

I sat there. I couldn't see what was going on below: the foliage was too dense. I heard voices and car doors slam. I recognised Savanto's voice, but I didn't understand what he was saying. He was speaking in Spanish. A harsh voice I hadn't heard before answered him. I guessed this would be Lopez, the witness.

After some minutes, I heard movements on the roof. The conversation was all in Spanish. I listened for Timoteo's voice, but didn't hear it. He was still doing his zombie act. Then after more talk, I heard the scrape of feet on the wooden ladder. I guessed they were going down, leaving Timoteo alone. I looked at my strap watch. The time was now 14.45. In another quarter of an hour Diaz would come out on to the bay ... providing he was coming.

Sweat was running down my face. I thought of the shot. I thought of lining this man's head up in the cross wires of the sight. I thought of the flattened sound from the silencer as I squeezed the trigger. I thought of seeing him drop into the sea with a hole in his head.

I sat motionless, listening. I heard nothing. Was someone still up on the roof with Timoteo? I didn't dare move until I was sure he was alone.

Then I heard his voice, pitched low. It just reached me.

'Mr. Benson...'

A child bleating for its mother, I thought savagely, then just as I was about to start my climb down, I froze.

Coiled up on the branch immediately below me was a diamondback rattler snake, its forked tongue flickering at my foot that was within twelve inches of it.

A diamondback rattler, one of the few deadly snakes in Florida, and it looked ready to strike!

*

'Mr. Benson...?'

Timoteo's whisper floated up to me.

I couldn't be sure if the sound of my voice would make the snake strike. I held my leg rigid, feeling the sweat of fear start out on me. I have always had a horror of snakes: even harmless snakes make my flesh creep. I looked down at this coiled horror. The shot, Diaz, Timoteo and even Lucy were washed out of my mind. I just sat astride the branch, motionless and cringing. My guts had gone away like a fist becoming a hand.

'Mr. Benson...'

A little louder ... more urgent.

'There's a snake up here.'

There was no power in my voice: it was a croaking whisper. He couldn't possibly have heard me, but the snake lifted its spade-shaped head. Its warning rattle, like dried beans shaken in a bag, made me flinch.

I sat there. I could hear voices talking in excited Spanish. I could hear the wind rustling in the palm trees. I stared down at the snake. Cramp was setting in in my legs.

'Mr. Benson...'

I knew the speed of a rattler strike. I hadn't a chance if I tried to get my legs up on to the branch. Besides, if I made such a wild movement, I could easily overbalance and crash down on the roof of the house.

'Snake,' I said, lifting my voice.

Again came the warning rattle.

Had Timoteo heard? If he had what would he do?

Minutes like hours dragged by. Then another sound came to me: the sound of a motorboat starting up. Even in my panic, half my mind switched to Lucy. My target was coming out on to the bay and here I was, treed by a snake!

Then I saw Timoteo. He was climbing awkwardly and very cautiously. He still had on his sun goggles and still wore the big black hat.

'Watch it!' I whispered. 'It's by my foot.'

Again the warning rattle: a sound that made my heart skip a beat.

About six feet below me, Timoteo paused. He peered up. I could see myself reflected in his sun goggles: a frightened, sweating man, cut down to size by a coiled reptile.

I could see by the way Timoteo stiffened that he had spotted the snake and that the snake had spotted him. It turned its head away from my foot and its forked tongue flickered in Timoteo's direction.

'Don't move,' Timoteo said quietly.

I had been about to snatch my leg out of range, but his quiet, confident tone stopped me.

Very slowly, he hoisted himself up to another branch. He was now within four feet of the snake.

I watched him, sweat rolling off me, my heart slamming against my ribs.

Very slowly, his hand began to move towards his hat.

The warning rattle sounded again.

His long fingers closed on the brim of his hat and slowly removed it from his head.

Simultaneously two things happened. The snake struck as Timoteo flicked the hat in its direction.

Scarcely breathing, I watched.

The snake's fangs sank into the felt brim of the hat. Timoteo, with a speed that almost defeated my eyes, had the snake off the branch. His right hand caught the snake at the back of its head. The length of the snake immediately wrapped itself around his arm. He sat astride the branch, just below me, gripping the back of the snake's head so it couldn't strike him, then his left hand came down on the spade-shaped head, his long fingers shutting the jaws. He paused. I could see the snake's body tight around his arm. Then firmly and deliberately, he turned his hands in the opposite direction, breaking the snake's back.

As he let the thin rope of snake flesh drop out of his hands, he looked up at me.

'It's dead.'

I sat with my back pressed against the trunk of the tree, looking down at him. I saw myself in the sun goggles and what I saw I didn't like.

Then the roar of the motor-boat snapped me back to life.

'Get down!' I said. 'Fast!'

Even before he began to climb down, I slid around him, dropping from one branch to another until I reached the roof. I grabbed up the rifle, spread myself flat under the shade of the shelter I had built and dug the rifle butt into my shoulder.

The motorboat was now in the bay. I could see the negress at the wheel. Nancy and a man were skiing side by side, but he was on her off-side and through the telescopic sight, she was shielding him.

When they turned, I thought, he would be on my side and I would have him.

I adjusted the focus. Every so often I caught a glimpse of him in the sight. He was a typical South American male sex symbol: well-built, muscular, handsome with long black hair held in place by a white bandeau.

The boat made a sharp turn and began the return run.

She and he were proving to each other how good they were. As the boat turned, he jumped her tow rope, skidding along on one ski and he was again on her off-side.

I waited, following them through the sight. I had the girl's head between the cross wires more often than Diaz's. It was an impossible shot. I could more easily kill her than him. They were now holding on to their tow bars with one hand and holding each other's hand with the other. They were now so close together I couldn't even see him on her off-side.

I lay there, sweating, but patient. I had been trained to wait. I had once waited three hours before I got a head shot and I remembered that while I waited.

The boat was coming round again. This time he kept to the on-side. They were doing a straight run. I now had his head on the cross wires. I could just see Nancy's nose and chin on the edge of the sight.

To anyone but an expert this would have been too dangerous. To anyone but an expert this could mean hitting the girl and not the man, but I was an expert.

This is it, I thought, this finishes the nightmare even if it starts another.

I drew in a long, slow breath, moving the sight to keep his head in the centre of the cross wires, then I slowly took up the slack of the trigger.

Suddenly, Nancy dropped back a little and she disappeared out of the sight. I knew then I had him. He wasn't even jinking. It was such a straightforward shot that Timoteo could have made it.

I squeezed the trigger.

Faintly, above the roar of the motorboat engine, I heard the metallic snap of the hammer in the gun. There was no recoil and that told me there was no cartridge in the breech. For a long stupefied moment I lay there, then I slammed down the loading lever which should jack up another cartridge under the firing-pin. The feel of the lever as it operated told me it wasn't lifting a cartridge.

I realised then the gun wasn't loaded. I had loaded it. I had had a cartridge in the breech, now it was unloaded.

I turned on my side and looked back at Timoteo who was standing away from me. I remembered the time lag before he had called to me: a time lag when he had been on the roof alone.

'Did you unload this gun, you sonofabitch?'

He nodded.

I looked out at the bay.

The two skiers were now well out of range, the boat taking them out to sea. I knew the opportunity had gone and the nightmare was still with me.

I got to my feet and walked over to him. I wanted to smash him flat, but there was no point. I told myself there was still tomorrow.

'Are you so goddam gutless you can't even let me kill this man for you?' I said, my voice low and savage.

Hidden behind the sun goggles, he faced me.

'You could say that, Mr. Benson,' he said huskily.

'Give me the clip.'

He took the clip of cartridges from his hip pocket and dropped it into my outstretched hand.

I looked at the bay. The skiers were out of sight, but I could still hear the drone of the motor-boat.

'Go down and talk yourself out of it,' I said. 'You're supposed to be a good talker. You'd better be convincing if Lucy means anything to you.'

He turned away and went down the ladder into the house.

In a few moments there came an explosion of talk in Spanish. I could hear Savanto's voice, quivering with rage. I had never heard him talk this way and although I didn't understand what he was saying the sound of the rage in his voice chilled me.

Every now and then I heard Timoteo say something. His voice was low-pitched and controlled among the other shouting voices. This went on for some time, then I heard car doors slam and cars start up.

There was a further long wait, then Raimundo came up the ladder. He paused when he saw me sitting on the parapet and he beckoned.

'Mr. Savanto wants you.'

I followed him down the ladder and out on to the verandah.

Savanto was sitting in a chair. Carlo was standing at the end of the verandah. He grinned idiotically at me. I went straight to Savanto. I took the clip of cartridges from my pocket and dropped it on the table in front of him.

'Your gutless son unloaded the gun while I was in the tree,' I said. 'It was a certain shot. He would be dead by now if your gutless son hadn't deliberately fouled up the operation.'

Savanto stared stonily at me.

'You should have checked the gun.'

'You think so? I had checked the gun. It was ready to shoot. Do you think I should have thought your son would have unloaded the gun? Would you have imagined he would unload the gun? Are you all that smart? The gun was ready to shoot. If you want to kick someone, kick your goddam son, not me!'

Savanto nodded.

'I have spoken to him. At least, he was convincing. Lopez believes the shot was impossible. From where we were watching, it looked that way. So we do it tomorrow.'

'This is tough enough without having to cope with your son.'

'You will have no further problems with him,' Savanto said. 'Just be certain, Mr. Benson, I have no problems with you.'

He turned to Carlo and held out his fat hand. Grinning, Carlo took from his hip pocket a flat packet carefully done up in tissue paper.

Savanto took it and laid it on the table.

'Here is something, Mr. Benson, to help you to be successful tomorrow. It could be something not so easily replaced next time. Please remember that.'

He got to his feet and followed by Carlo, he went down to the Cadillac.

I hesitated for a long moment before I went to the table. The Cadillac drove away as Raimundo came up to me.

'Leave it, soldier,' he said quietly. 'It's her hair. He had it cut off, but she's all right, soldier. He just wants you to know he means business.'

I stared at him.

'Her hair?'

He turned away.

'It'll grow again.'

With shaking hands I opened the packet. The sight of Lucy's golden tresses, tied neatly into a switch with black ribbon, made my heart lurch.

'When did this happen?' I said, scarcely recognising my voice.

'This morning.'

I sat down. I had to. Suddenly there was no strength in my legs. I touched the hair, feeling its softness.

'This morning? When you went for the whisky?'

'No ... after. I told you she was all right. It was after.'

'Does Timoteo know about this?'

'Not then. Now he's back, he'll know.'

I folded the tissue paper around the switch. I couldn't bear to look at it any more.

'I'm sorry, soldier,' Raimundo said quietly.

I turned in the chair. He was standing with his back against one of the verandah's uprights. His dark, sweating face looked troubled. His eyes shifted as they met mine.

'Do you go along with this?' I asked. 'Do you okay this . . .?' I put my hands on the tissue paper. 'And this?' I let my shirt fall open so that he could see the Red Dragon brand. 'Do you think a man who can do things like this could be the saviour of peasants?'

He lifted his shoulders.

'He gets things done, soldier. This is what counts. To get things done, he acts mean from time to time.' He wiped the sweat off his face with the back of his hand. 'He has done a lot of good. Ten years ago, his people had to haul water in cans two miles to their homes. He said he would fix that. They didn't believe him. He found out a politician was having it off with his own daughter. Don't ask me how he found out . . . that's his gift . . . to find out the weakness of men. He talked to this politician. You can call it blackmail if you want to, but water pipes were laid on. Not so long ago all the stuff our people grew had to be taken into town by mules. I used to drive some of the mules. Savanto decided we should have trucks. There was another politician.' He shrugged. 'Savanto found out something about him. They talked and ten trucks appeared. This is the way he works.' He spread his hands helplessly. 'If he wants something for his people, he gets it and he doesn't give a goddam how he gets it.'

'Do these peasants know the kind of man he is?'

'Some of them guess; some of them could know; most of them are too grateful to ask questions.'

'And you?' I stared at him.

Raimundo pushed himself away from the verandah support. 'I'm taking a swim. Do you want to come with me?'

I shook my head.

'It'll work out, soldier. Up to now, he has always kept his word.'

'Up to now.'

He went down the steps, across the sand dunes and towards the sea.

I put my hand on the packet of tissue paper, then I unwrapped it and released the soft tresses.

Stroking the long, blonde hair brought me very close to Lucy.

The idea of how to solve this nightmare came to me. It suddenly dropped into my mind and I wondered why I had been so dumb not to have thought of it before.

I looked down at the blonde tresses on the table, then at the Red Dragon brand on my chest.

Savanto had said to me: *How many men have you killed in coldblood? Eighty-two? What is one more life to you?*

I would probably have to kill Diaz.

Life eighty-three.

I knew for certain now that I would kill Augusto Savanto.

Life eighty-four.

But that would be a pleasure.

*

I was still sitting on the verandah when Raimundo came back from his swim.

During the half hour I had been alone, my mind had been active.

Raimundo looked uneasily at me as he came up the steps. His eyes strayed to the switch of hair lying on the table.

'Why don't you take a swim?' he said, pausing at the head of the steps. 'It's good in there.'

I shook my head, keeping my expression deadpan. I didn't want him to suspect what was going on in my mind.

'It's too hot right now. Maybe later,' I said.

He nodded and went into the house to change out of his trunks.

I again touched Lucy's hair, then wrapped the switch in the tissue paper and put it in my hip pocket.

Then somewhere in the house I heard the telephone bell start up. I heard Raimundo thumping down the stairs to answer it.

I switched my mind back to Augusto Savanto. I wondered how long he would stay at the Imperial Hotel. He would probably leave after Diaz was dead. I pictured him sitting on the balcony on the fourteenth floor of the hotel which faced the sea. At the end of the boulevard was a twenty-storey block of apartments still under construction. The syndicate building it had run out of money, and for the time being construction had stopped although it was nearly finished. Lucy and I, spending a day in Paradise City, had visited the building. We had nothing better to do and a sign over the entrance invited inspection. We had been pop-eyed at the rentals they were asking. The penthouse apartment on the 20th floor had been luxuriously furnished and just for the hell of it, we had taken the elevator up on the long ride to look at it. The agent, showing us round, had spotted we had no money, but as he had nothing better to do he had gone along with us. Standing on the terrace of the penthouse, I remembered, I had had a clear view of the Imperial Hotel.

If I could get up there with the Weston & Lees, I would have no problem in putting a bullet in the middle of Savanto's evil head. This is what I wanted to do and was now determined to do.

My thoughts were interrupted as Raimundo came flying out on to the verandah.

I have become used to seeing frightened faces. When you go into battle the times I have you are often surrounded by faces that telegraph fear. I immediately recognised the signs.

'Timoteo and your wife have bolted!' His voice was unnaturally loud. 'We've got to find them!'

For a brief moment I couldn't believe what he was saying, then I jumped to my feet, kicking away my chair.

'Bolted? Where? What the hell are you saying?'

He gulped, then steadied himself.

'Nick just phoned. Timoteo and your wife took off for the Cypress swamp! You've got to help me find them!'

He charged down the steps, bawling for Carlo as he pounded across the sand to the Volkswagen.

Carlo appeared around the back of the house, running flat footed, his brutish face bewildered.

Raimundo came to a skidding stop by the car and looked back at me.

'Come on!' he yelled. 'Come on!'

By the time I reached the car, Carlo was in the back seat and Raimundo had the car on the move. As I slammed the door shut, he took off, skidding over the sand, then he raced the car down the narrow road so we heaved and banged over the bumps while he wrestled with the wheel.

We finally reached the highway. None of us could speak while we had rushed down the sandy lane. It was as much as we could do to hold ourselves in our seats.

As the smooth tarmac of the highway slid under the wheels, I said, 'How did they get away?'

'Timoteo went berserk when he saw your wife had lost her hair,' Raimundo said savagely. 'He flattened Nick. He tried to get her to the highway but the other guards headed him off.

They bolted into the Cypress swamp. The guards followed them as far as it was safe, then they turned back, but they have them bottled up. We have to go in there and get them out.'

As a back-drop to the swank villas along the beach, the Cypress swamp was a twenty-thousand acre jungle, waiting to be reclaimed. When I had first come to Paradise City, I had optimistically gone into the swamp after wild duck. I had found it a jungle of cypress trees and red, white and black mangroves, their roots like elephant tusks. Grey Spanish moss, duckweed and bladderwort, festooning the trees, offered hiding places for snakes, giant spiders and scorpions. The swamp was interlaced with narrow canals of stagnant water covered with white lilies and a breeding place for mosquitoes. Step wrong and you could sink to your death in evil-smelling slime. It was a hell of a place to get lost in.

Nick Lewis had a flat-bottomed boat which he had turned over to me. I had used it once to navigate the canals, but after being practically eaten alive by mosquitoes, and seeing a crocodile that, luckily for me, was too lazy and well fed to charge the boat, I had quit. I had laid up the boat and given up the idea of shooting wild duck.

The thought of Lucy being in this hell hole with a numbskull like Timoteo sent a rush of blood to my head.

'We've got to find them!' Raimundo was shouting. 'If Savanto hears of this, none of us will live!'

'That's fine ... the saviour of peasants,' I said. 'Are you putting me on or do you mean it?'

'I mean it!'

His set face and the panic in his eyes told me he did mean it.

It took us less than a quarter of an hour to reach the villa I had seen from Nancy's boat. We tore down the dirt road and came to a tyre-screaming stop at the front entrance.

Nick, in his yellow-and-red Hawaiian shirt, was waiting for us. The side of his jaw was swollen and he looked like a man facing sudden death. He burst into a stream of frantic Spanish as Raimundo tumbled out of the car. I got out and Carlo followed me, his brutish face glistening with sweat. As I couldn't understand what Nick was bawling about, I moved away and stood waiting in the shade.

Raimundo cut Nick short and came over to me.

'Have you ever been in the swamp, soldier?' he asked.

'No.'

It was a lie I felt sure would pay off.

'They're in there and they can't get out. Three of our boys are guarding the exits. We'll join up with them and flush them out.'

It took us some ten minutes, walking fast in the broiling sun to reach the edge of the swamp. There was a narrow path that led into the swamp, and here we found the man in the white ducks, waiting. After talking to him in Spanish, Raimundo told me it was along this path that Timoteo and Lucy had entered the swamp.

'This is your kind of territory, soldier,' he went on. 'You lead the way in.'

I knew what was ahead. The path went into the swamp for something like a quarter of a mile, then it petered out. From then on it was bog, jungle, canals and mosquitoes.

I started down the path with Raimundo close on my heels. Behind him came Nick, Carlo and the man in the white ducks. It was steamy hot in there and the smell of decay, stagnant water and rotting vegetation increased as we penetrated further into the jungle.

I had spent three years in similar jungles. My eyes were trained to see things which the men following me were blind to. A broken branch, a smudge on the mud-packed path, disturbed leaves told me this was the way they had come.

Finally, we reached the end of the path. We stood in a group, looking at the dense jungle ahead of us, divided by a ten-foot-wide canal with its beautiful floating lilies.

'We'll split up here,' I said. 'Two men to the left: two to the right. I'll go straight ahead.'

Raimundo shook his head.

'I'm staying with you, soldier. You're not going it alone.'

I hadn't expected it would be that easy.

'Okay. Get these guys going.'

He sent Carlo and the man in the white ducks to the far side of the canal and Nick on his own to the right.

When we were alone, Raimundo turned to face me.

'Don't try any tricks, soldier,' he said. 'We have got to find them and bring them back. Listen to me! Savanto has an organisation of killers! They can reach you and your wife wherever you try to hide. I'm warning you! No one has ever double-crossed him and survived. If we don't bring them back, you and I are dead men.'

'So let's go and find them,' I said.

Not if Savanto has a hole in his head, I thought.

I moved into the jungle. Some five hundred yards ahead of me was Nick Lewis's old boat, completely hidden by the dense undergrowth. Three months ago I had dragged it out of the canal on to the bank. There was no reason why it shouldn't be there still. I was sure my only chance of finding Lucy was to use the boat. They couldn't have got far into the swamp and they were probably hiding somewhere along the canal. But Raimundo was in my way. I knew he was alert. I had to put him out of action before I reached the boat.

Ahead of us I saw a dense obstruction of mangrove roots. I stopped. Mosquitoes hummed around my head as I turned.

Faintly, I could hear the other men crashing their way through the jungle. I couldn't see them and that meant they couldn't see us.

'They can't have come this way,' I said. 'They wouldn't get through here. We'd better go back.'

Raimundo slashed at the mosquitoes that were tormenting him.

'Anything you say . . .?'

I braced myself, shifting my feet so that I was on perfect balance.

'Watch it!' The snap in my voice startled him. 'Snake!' and I pointed at his feet.

As his eyes shifted away from me, I slammed a punch at his jaw. I should have remembered how fast he was. Even though I had him fooled for a split second, he was fast enough to shift his head a fraction. It was enough. My fist scraped along his face, throwing him off balance, but it wasn't the killer punch I had intended. I hit him with my left as he struggled to stay upright and he went down. But he was very much alive . . . too alive. His legs gripped mine and I came down on top of him. My hands went to his throat. It was like holding on to a savage trapped animal. His fist smashed into my mouth. The power behind the punch threw me off him. He was struggling up on to his knees as I kicked out at him: my foot slammed into his chest, throwing him down again. I pounced on him, my hands seeking his throat. Again his fist banged into my face, but this time I held on. I felt the muscles in my shoulders and arms turn into knots as I exerted all my strength into my fingers. His legs began to thrash. He tried to reach my face with hooked fingers, but his strength was leaving him. Savagely, I increased my grip. He stared up at me, his eyes sightless, then his legs stopped moving, his mouth opened and his tongue came out and blood started to run from his nostrils.

As he went limp, I released my grip and got away from him. I could see the imprint of my fingers on his throat. I wasn't sure if he was dead or alive, and I didn't care. I had had enough of Savanto and his thugs. They had come into my life and had disrupted it, now I was at last hitting back.

My nose was bleeding slightly and my lips were swelling. Mosquitoes plagued me. I didn't give a goddam. Somewhere in this stinking jungle I was going to find Lucy. That's all I had on my mind.

Leaving Raimundo lying on the hard-packed mud, I started off to find the boat. I found it where I had left it, high and dry on the bank. As I heaved it down to the water a spider as big as my fist scuttled out of it: an obscene thing with short legs as thick as my finger, covered with black hair.

After a struggle, I got the boat into the water, then I climbed in, picking up the pole. I began the slow punt up the canal. As I forced the boat through the weeds and the water lilies the mosquitoes struck at me and the steamy heat was like a jacket of cotton wool around me.

I struggled on for something like an hour. I had been trained by the Army to withstand mosquitoes and heat. I was savagely determined to find Lucy and it was a challenge my body was ready to accept.

Then I saw them.

I saw Timoteo first. He was sitting with his back to a tree in a small clearing by the canal. A cloud of mosquitoes swarmed around his head. Lying across his knees was Lucy. He was fanning her with his hat.

She lay limply, her shirt and white slacks plastered to her body, her cropped blonde head lying on his knee, showing the lovely line of her throat.

He saw me as I forced the boat through the overhanging branches of the mangrove trees.

I saw his hands go around her: the action of a child whose favourite toy is threatened.

She lifted her head and saw me.

I saw fear appear on her mud-stained face. She clutched hold of Timoteo, then she frantically waved at me, as if by the wave of her hand she could make me vanish.

Chapter Eight

I dug the pole into the slime, a cold, murderous rage exploding inside me, and heaved the punt forward. The blunt prow hit the bank and slid up it. I dropped the pole into the boat and jumped on to the bank.

Lucy, looking terrified, backed away, leaving Timoteo to face me. I charged up the steep bank like an enraged bull, intent only on getting my hands around his throat, but the slime of the bank beat me. My feet slipped when I was within reach of him and I sprawled face down with a thud that drove the breath out of my body.

If I had been Timoteo, I would have put the boot in. A solid kick to the head would have finished me, but he remained motionless in that exasperating zombie stance of his while I tried to get to my feet in the oozing slime. As I struggled, he bent forward, caught hold of my arm and with surprising strength, heaved me upright. Blind with fury, I swung at him, but the unbalanced swing made my feet slide from under me and cursing, I slid down the bank to splash into the stagnant water.

Spluttering, I surfaced, tearing weeds and water-lily leaves from my face. I was up to my waist in the warm, stinking water. My feet sank into the mud of the canal bottom, like wet concrete, and I found myself trapped.

'Leave him!' I heard Lucy scream. 'Tim! Come away!'

The effect of those words was like a bucket of iced water poured over me. My rage sparked out. I remained fixed in the mud, realising that what I had already suspected was true. Timoteo slid down the bank and into the boat. Leaning forward, he offered me his hand. For a moment I hesitated, then I caught hold of his wrist. With scarcely an effort, he heaved me out of the mud and into the boat, steadying the boat as it threatened to overturn.

'Tim! He'll kill you!' Lucy screamed frantically.

As I got to my feet, I saw her sliding down the bank, a stick in her hand. She missed the boat and landed in the water. As Timoteo and I both reached out to grab her, the boat capsized, throwing us into the water beside her.

I was the first to reach her. As I pulled her upright, she hit me across the face with the stick. The wood was rotten and flew into bits as it struck me.

Frantically, she splashed away from me as Timoteo reached

her. I felt my feet beginning to sink in the mud. Somehow, I struggled to the bank, caught hold of a tree root and dragged myself on to firm ground.

Timoteo had Lucy in his arms, but I saw he was sinking. I hung on to the tree and reached out my hand. He caught hold of it and I dragged them to the side of the bank. He heaved Lucy up to me, then as she rolled away from me, I helped him on to the bank.

For some moments we lay there, trying to breathe, the sweat pouring off us, the mosquitoes making a cloud around us.

I thought of the rotten stick breaking across my face and I looked at Lucy who was lying on her back, her hands covering her face. Then I sat up and looked at Timoteo who was scraping mud out of his eyes.

'So besides being a gutless bastard,' I said, 'you now have become a wife stealer.'

Lucy struggled up.

'I love him!' she screamed at me. 'He isn't gutless. He's wonderful! You don't . . .'

'Oh, shut up!' I barked at her.

She flinched away from me as I continued to stare at Timoteo.

'Lucy and I love each other,' he said quietly.

'And you shut up!'

I slithered down the bank into the water. As I began to struggle to right the boat, Timoteo joined me. Together, we got the boat floating again. As I climbed into the boat, he pulled himself up on to the bank to join Lucy.

I looked up at them.

'We can get through to the sea,' I said. 'Do you want to come or do you want to go on with your goddam Romeo and Juliet act?'

They slid down the bank to the boat. I watched Timoteo as he half carried, half led Lucy down the slippery bank. I realised his hands had a tenderness that mine could never have.

She sat at the far end of the boat, away from me. The sight of her cropped head and the unhappiness on her face sent a pang through me.

Timoteo moved to the middle of the boat and sat down on the cross bench.

I picked up the pole and began to force the boat through the weeds. I had been doing this for the past hour before I had found them. With their extra weight, I now found it a struggle to move the boat.

I struggled on, sweat pouring off me, then finally with my heart hammering, my breath hissing through my clenched teeth, I stopped, leaning on the pole beaten.

'I'll do it.'

Timoteo stood up and took the pole.

I hated to be beaten, but I couldn't go on. I sank down on the bench and dropped my head into my sweating, blistered hands.

He had either a lot more strength than I or he had the knack I hadn't got, but he kept the boat moving through the weeds at a speed I didn't think possible.

Finally, we broke out of the weeds and into salt water after an hour's gruelling struggle. By then I had my strength back and I took the pole from Timoteo's exhausted hands. Now it was his turn to slump down on the bench.

Minutes later, we were free from the torment of the mosquitoes and I could see the jungle opening up and ahead of us, the sea. Another ten minutes brought us out into the light of the evening sun: a red ball as it sank below the horizon. There was no longer any need to use the pole: the current took us along towards the open sea. As the boat drifted away from the overhanging branches of the mangrove trees, I dropped the pole into the boat and flopped down behind Timoteo on the forward bench.

Finally, the prow of the boat bumped into a sand bank, slewed around and came to rest.

Not bothering about the other two, I stripped off my wet, mud-caked shirt and dived into the sea. I swam slowly, feeling the mud, the blood and the sweat leaving my body.

I love him!

A woman doesn't scream that at the husband she has lived with for only six months in that tone of voice unless she means it. This wasn't hysteria. I knew I had lost Lucy.

When I felt clean enough, I swam back to the boat. I swam slowly. I saw Timoteo and Lucy were also in the sea. I trod water, watching them. After a while they came out of the sea and moved up the beach to a sand dune.

I came out of the sea and walked up to them.

Timoteo got to his feet while Lucy sat where she was, staring up at me, her eyes round and terrified.

'Okay, slob,' I said, pausing in front of him. 'Maybe you can't shoot, but you can steal my wife. Tell me, how many times have you screwed her?'

He didn't react as I hoped he would. I had hoped to provoke

him to take a swing at me and then it would have been a knock down and drag out which I wanted.

'Did my father do that to you?' he asked in a shocked, husky whisper.

I saw he was looking at the Red Dragon brand.

'Does that bother you?' I said. 'Does that bother you more than stealing my wife? Your father isn't fit to live. I'm going to kill him.' I moved around so that I stood in front of Lucy. She jumped to her feet, backing away from me.

'Look at this, Lucy,' I said, pointing to the brand. 'His father said he would put this on your face if I didn't kill a man this slob is too gutless to kill. He branded me to show me he meant business. Do you still want this gutless creep who hasn't the guts to spit in the face of the animal who calls himself his father? Do you?'

She stared with horror at the brand mark, then she put her hands to her face.

'Lucy! Do you want me or do you want him?' I yelled at her.

I saw by the expression in her eyes that I had lost her.

'I'm sorry, Jay ... We love each other.'

I slapped her face. As she reeled back, I saw Timoteo move. I spun around and into a punch that lifted me off my feet and flung me down on my back with my head half in the sea.

I wanted this. I was sure I could take him. I wanted to smash him and drop him bleeding and helpless at Lucy's feet. I wanted to show her the kind of man she had chosen.

I had had a number of fights when I was in the Army. Every so often you got a challenge: some guy would think he was better than you and you had to show him he was wrong. Sometimes a guy was nearly right and the fight was long, bloody and savage. I had had around twenty fights while I was in the Army and I lost only one. This guy I had lost to had a chest like a beer barrel and I had broken my hands on him. He took everything I gave him: grinning, his face a mask of blood. I got one of his teeth embedded in my fist and I broke two fingers of my left hand hanging a punch on his jaw. He took everything I dished out and he still stayed on his feet. Then when I had nothing else to throw at him, he started to creep towards me like a crab and started hitting me. Well, he was a better fighter and a lot stronger than I was, and when he finally stretched me on my back, covered with blood, I admitted it.

But I was sure Timoteo wasn't a better and stronger fighter than I was, but I had learned he could punch and he was fast so

I moved towards him cautiously. I wanted to land one crippling punch and once I had him shaken, I would go in and cut him to pieces: that's what I wanted to do.

I moved in, weaving, my head down, my chin tucked in, feinting with my left to set him up for my right. It was the classic Jack Dempsey attack, but he wasn't there. As my right started, he slid away. With the ease of a professional, he caught me with a short jolting right that exploded on the side of my jaw and stretched me flat on my back.

I had walked into the punch and worse, I hadn't seen it coming. Then I knew I was up against a fighter who might lick me.

I felt a trickle of blood run down my chin. I wiped it away with the back of my hand, shook my head and got to my feet.

Timoteo stood away from me, his long arms hanging by his sides, his serious, goddam intellectual face expressionless.

I started towards him. He let me come within punching distance, then with the same professional arrogance, he slid my rush and again I found myself flat on my back from a bruising punch to the side of my head. This long slob carried a punch like the kick of a mule.

I stared up at him. He had again moved back and was looking down at me. Behind him I could see Lucy watching, her eyes large and her hands to her face.

'You're quite a fighter, aren't you, you sonofabitch?' I said as I got to my feet. 'Well, so am I.'

He could dish it out, but could he take it? I knew I could absorb a lot of punishment. I was built to take it, but could this thin beanpole take a man-sized punch?

He seemed rooted to the sand until I got within range of him, then he flitted away. He poked out a long left that thudded into my face and rocked me back.

Go ahead, slob, I thought, and I kept coming in to be jabbed away with long raking lefts. Up to now I hadn't landed a punch on him, and I had taken half a dozen jolts, but I had taken such punches before. I again bored in. The left jab came again, but this time I was ready for it. I shifted and closed in. I hit him in the belly with all I had. I felt my fist sink in. I heard the breath come out of him like the sound of a burst tyre. I saw his face fall to pieces and I smashed my right to his jaw. He went down as if pole-axed. I stood over him, my chest heaving, blood from the cuts he had made in my face dripping on my chest.

Lucy ran between us and kneeling down, she lifted his head and cradled it against her breasts.

I watched her for a long moment, then I turned and walked down the sandbank into the sea.

I had a long swim ahead of me, but I was in the mood for a long swim.

*

The moon was coming up behind the palm trees as I came out of the sea. I had three things to do: I had to get a change of clothes; I had to pick up my car, and then I had to drive to the little white house and pick up the Weston & Lees rifle.

The villa where Lucy had been was in darkness, but I approached it cautiously. I moved through the flowering shrubs until I got round to the front of the house, then I paused to listen. I heard nothing. In the light of the moon I could see my Volkswagen parked where Raimundo had left it.

Nick and the other guards had been living in the place. In there, I would find a change of clothes. Although it was a temptation to jump into the car and drive away, I had to get out of my mud-stained, soaking-wet slacks and put on other clothes.

I found the front door unlocked. I moved into the darkness silently. I found the stairs and climbed them, listening, cautious all the time. The first door I opened led into a bathroom. The light from the moon was strong enough now for me to find my way around without turning on any lights. The second door led into a bedroom. There I found what I was looking for: dark slacks and a black sweat-shirt. The fit was tight but good enough. I also found with some impatient searching a pair of stout, leather-soled sandals. Holding the sandals in my hand, I crept down the stairs, paused at the front door to put the sandals on, then crossed the tarmac to the Volkswagen. I found the key in the ignition lock. With my heart banging against my ribs, I started the engine, engaged gear and drove down the drive.

No one shouted after me. When I reached the narrow road, I turned on the headlights and stamped down on the gas pedal.

It took me under fifteen minutes to reach the road leading to the little white house. Here, I stopped the car, turned off the lights and walked the rest of the way.

Reaching the house, I saw it was in darkness, but even then I took my time approaching it.

The rifle was up on the roof where I had left it. Moving as silently as I knew how, I went up the steps of the verandah and moved into the dark house, pausing to listen. I heard nothing so

I went on up the stairs to the ladder that led to the roof, lit by the brilliant white moon.

Raimundo was sitting on the parapet, a colt automatic pistol in his hand: its blunt nose pointing at me.

'I've been waiting for you, soldier,' he said. His voice was husky and I could see in the light of the moon his throat was swollen. 'I thought you'd be along to collect the rifle. No tricks unless you want a second navel. Sit over there.'

I rubbed my hand across my bruised, mosquito-bitten face and then walked over to the parapet about five yards from him and sat down.

I had tricked him once before and given time I could trick him again, but did I have the time?

As I sat down, he lowered the gun, resting it on his thigh. His left hand went to his throat.

'You goddam nearly killed me,' he said.

'What did you expect?'

'Don't let's waste time. Savanto knows Timoteo and your wife got away. You know what that means, soldier?'

'You told me. We're dead men.'

'That's it. Did you find them?'

'I found them. She and he are doing a modern Romeo and Juliet act.'

He stared at me.

'Those were the characters who died young . . . or is my education slipping?'

'They were the two.'

He continued to stare at me.

'I don't know if I'm with you, soldier. Are you telling me Timoteo has stolen your wife?'

'That's about right, but it isn't one-sided.'

He touched his throat gingerly as he thought.

'Doesn't seem to be your lucky day, does it?'

Probably it was his way of saying he was sorry.

'Any cigarettes?' I asked.

He tossed me a pack and a book of matches. I lit up and as I made to throw them back, he said, 'Keep them; the way my throat feels I can't imagine I'll ever smoke again.'

'You had it coming.'

He grinned crookedly.

'I was holding on to the last pieces. Where are they?'

'Where you won't find them.'

'I don't want to.' Again he touched his throat. 'But Savanto will find them. He'll find you and me too.'

I didn't say anything. I was tempted to say that I would find Savanto first, but I wasn't sure if that kind of talk would pay dividends.

I watched Raimundo lay the pistol on the parapet by his side. I decided he was too fast, even slowed down by a swollen throat, for me to jump him.

'It won't be long, soldier, before they come here and find us,' he said. 'Then there will be some shooting. Then you and I will be dropped into the sea. Then they will go after Timoteo and your wife and there will be more shooting and they will be dropped into the swamp.'

I regarded him. His face was glistening with sweat. He looked like a man waiting to die.

'Are you telling me Savanto would have his own son murdered?'

Raimundo wiped his mouth with the back of his hand.

'He has to. The word has gone out that his son has walked over his father's face. That's the way these people talk. No one walks across the face of the Boss and survives, even if he is the Boss's son. If the old man is to remain Boss, Timoteo will have to go, and the old man is going to remain Boss, make no mistake about that.'

'Boss of what? Boss of a lot of peasants? Is that all that important to him?'

Raimundo hesitated, then shrugged.

'Why shouldn't you know? I'm out of the deal now. Savanto thinks big, makes big plans and makes big promises. All these goddam peasants he talks about look on him as God. So to stay God, he must have money: the kind of money you and I can't even imagine. His brother runs the Red Dragon organisation and this organisation has the money Savanto needs because they control the gambling and the drug traffic in Venezuela and that's where the big money is. Toni Savanto, the brother, is dying of cancer of the liver. He can't last much more than a couple of weeks ... if that. Diaz, his son, is a very smart cookie and his heir. So long as he is alive, Savanto hasn't a hope of taking over the Red Dragons. You would imagine nothing could be more simple than to knock Diaz off. The old man has only to tell me and I'd do it, but that's not the way he works. Because a quarter of a million, simple-minded, starving peasants look on him as God, and because he is also beginning to think he is God, he doesn't want it known he has blood on his hands. There are ten men known as the Elders who do the administrative work of the Little Brothers and Savanto is scared of them. They have the power, if they gang up on him, to ease him into retirement. These men would never go along with a killing, but they would go along with a vendetta. That's part of their tradition.' Raimundo paused as he stared out to sea, then he went on, 'So the old man's problem was how to get rid of Diaz. With Diaz out of the way, the Red Dragons would be like a fat, sleek body without a head. The old man has only to reach out and stick his head on the headless body to have all the money he needs to make good his promises. So he cooks up this idea of getting rid of Diaz and establishing Timoteo, who is his heir, as a guy to be taken seriously. Timoteo was told what to do. When Savanto tells anyone what to do, he does it. So Savanto found a girl and Timoteo took her around until the Elders were sold on the idea he was in love with her. I know Timoteo couldn't stand the sight of her, but he did what he was told. When the background was established, the girl was given a massive dose of something or other that killed her. Just before she died, Carlo branded her face with the Red Dragon symbol which was stolen from the old man's brother. Savanto called the Elders and showed them the girl's body. He told them Diaz had raped and branded her as a challenge to Timoteo. The Elders fell for it. They said Timoteo had to kill Diaz. They knew Savanto had only to give the sign and Diaz would be dead, but that would be murder. But if Timoteo killed him, that would be justice. So Savanto had to put on a show. He knew he couldn't force Timoteo to kill Diaz. Timoteo was a yes-man to a point, but he stopped at murder. So you got involved, I got involved, and now Timoteo has fouled it up by running away. That puts him in trouble. The Elders know by now what he has done and they have turned their thumbs down. If Savanto wants to remain boss, he has to turn his thumb down too. So Diaz gets a new lease of life and Timoteo is marked to be hit. Later, Savanto will cook up another idea to get rid of Diaz. He's full of those kind of ideas. So Savanto's button men are after Timoteo. They will knock off your wife, you and me because we know too much. We are all dead bodies ... make no mistake about that, soldier. The word has gone out.'

'What happens if Savanto drops dead?' I asked, flicking the butt of my cigarette into the darkness.

'He won't drop dead. He's built to last.'

'But suppose he does drop dead. What happens?'

Raimundo stiffened. He got the message.

'Timoteo would take over. The peasants wouldn't do so well but they would survive. But Savanto isn't going to drop dead.'

I lit another cigarette.

'I think it's time he did.'

We looked at each other.

'It can't be done, soldier,' Raimundo said, shaking his head. 'The red light has gone up. This is the first thing Savanto would think of now he knows the operation has turned sour. By now he is surrounded by his button men: men trained for just this job. Get that idea out of your mind.'

'Do you want to be in on this?' I asked. 'Or are you chickening out and sitting here waiting to be slaughtered?'

'You don't know what you're up against, soldier.'

'Haven't you the guts to try? What have you to lose?'

He hesitated.

'What do I do?'

'I'm going to kill this man,' I said. 'He came into my life with promises. Now you tell me he is going to kill my wife and kill me. Okay, I believe you. He branded me.' I put my fingers through my shirt opening and felt the scar on my chest. 'No man can regard himself as God. I don't give a damn if he is the father of a lot of starving peasants if this is the way he works. I don't believe these peasants would think anything of him if they knew the kind of animal he is. There is a hell of a lot of talk about tradition. Well, I have traditions too. No one brands me or threatens me and gets away with it. He called me a professional killer. I am just that.' I got to my feet. 'You tell me I'll be dead, but I tell you Savanto will be dead before me. I'm going to kill him!'

Raimundo shook his head.

'I go along with all you say, soldier, but you won't kill him. He is organised. Getting a shot at Diaz is kid's stuff to getting a shot at Savanto.'

I crossed the roof to where I had left the rifle and I picked it up.

'Listen to me, soldier,' Raimundo went on. 'No one can hope to knock off Savanto when he is alert, and now, he is very alert. He thinks ahead all the time. Do you imagine he doesn't know you will come after him? He knows now the set-up has turned sour. He knows Timoteo has taken off with your wife. He's smart. He knows you will be after his blood. How do you imagine he has survived for so long? Because he's lucky?' He took a cigarette from his pack that I had left on the parapet and lit it. 'This is going to kill me, but if I don't smoke I'll flip my lid.' He coughed like a man with lung cancer as soon as the smoke reached his sore throat and cursing, he threw the cigarette away. 'That's the way you and I will go, soldier ... like dead butts.' He waited a moment while he wheezed, then went on. 'He knows you will come after him. He is a judge of men. I've worked for him since I was a kid of fifteen and he is an expert in judging men, so he knows you now plan to fix him. But he has a trained organisation to take care of guys like you. He is up in his lush suite at the Imperial Hotel. He likes living there. The staff drop on their knees and beat their stupid heads on the carpet at the sight of him and he loves that. So a punk like you, soldier, won't shift him out, but he knows the danger points.' He gave a snorting, derisive laugh. 'You're aiming to nail him as he sits on the balcony of his suite, aren't you? You aim to use the apartment block across the way to get at him.'

'That's the way I'll get him,' I said.

Raimundo threw up his hands in despair.

'Do you imagine he hasn't thought of that? He thinks of everything.'

'I'll kill him from there.'

'You're just sounding off,' Raimundo said angrily. 'By now, that apartment block will be swarming with his button men. You'd never get within a hundred yards of it! That is the one place Savanto can be got at and that's why it will be made safe!'

I swung the rifle from one hand to the other.

'Because it is safe, it is the one place I can get at him,' I said.

Raimundo gaped at me.

'It's because he is sure and his men will be sure the place is safe that it ceases to be safe,' I said. 'They will be so damn sure it's safe they will be looking elsewhere for the action to start. There are twenty floors in this building with around fifteen rooms to a floor and each room is empty. That offers me three hundred hiding-places, apart from the corridors. How many men do you think will be guarding this block of apartments? At a guess, ten men who are quick on the trigger and very alert. Where will they be? Five of them will be covering the entrances. There will be a couple of men covering the elevators and there are certain to be at least two men on the top floor which overlooks the hotel. They will be so satisfied that the other guy is alert, they will cease to be alert after they have been at action stations for more than three or four hours. They will be no different from Army sentries and I know how they behave. I'm going to take a look at the place. Do you want to come?'

He remained sitting on the parapet for a long moment, then he got to his feet.

'What have I to lose? I still think you're crazy, but anything is better than sitting here, waiting for a bullet.'

'Have you any money?'

He cocked his head on one side.

'I've a couple of hundred in my room.'

'That'll do.'

As he started towards the trap door, I caught hold of his arm. 'You take the rifle. I'll go first. You wait here . . . I'll call you.'

I saw his eyes widen in the moonlight.

'You think they could be here already?' His voice sank to an uneasy whisper.

'They could be. From now on, I'm taking no chances. Give me your gun.'

He hesitated, then he picked up the automatic and handed it to me as I handed him the rifle.

I moved to the trap door and listened, then holding the gun in my hand, I swung myself down into the darkness. I heard nothing and nothing happened. It wasn't until I had been through the whole house, moving like a shadow, that I was satisfied that Raimundo and I were still on our own. I returned to the foot of the ladder and called to him.

He came down and I took the rifle from him.

'Get the money and a suitcase,' I said. 'We might have to go to a hotel.'

Ten minutes later we were heading for Paradise City.

*

The night porter of the Palm Court Hotel was an elderly negro who was sleeping peacefully behind the reception desk. The fly-blown clock behind his nodding head showed 02.22

We had had some luck. On our way to Paradise City we had come on a car with a bag of golf clubs in the rear seat. I had stood on the brake pedal and had nearly sent Raimundo's head through the windscreen.

This car had been parked outside an 'Eat-'n-Dance' joint, the kind that litter Highway 1 until you reach Paradise City.

'Get it!' I said.

Raimundo read my thoughts. He slid out of the Volkswagen, grabbed the golf bag, emptied the clubs on to the back seat and was back in the car within ten seconds.

So we arrived at the Palm Court Hotel with the Weston & Lees rifle hidden in the golf bag and a suitcase full of nothing: like two respectable guys on vacation.

The old negro came awake and blinked at us. After a lot of fumbling with the register, he found us a double room with twin beds on the second floor. We signed in as Toni Franchini and Harry Brewster. I told him we didn't know how long we'd stay and he didn't seem to care. He took us up in a creaking elevator, unlocked a door and showed us into a big, shabbily-furnished room. He had tried to take the suitcase and the golf bag, but when I told him I was giving my muscles some exercise, he gave me a dismal smile as if he were sure I was going to gyp him out of his tip. I gave him a dollar after he had proved the plumbing worked and he went away, happy.

I sat on the bed while Raimundo took the only armchair.

Before arriving at the hotel we had driven past the Imperial Hotel and past the apartment block, under construction. We had luck as the night traffic was heavy and we could crawl without attracting attention. We even got into a solid jam of cars right outside the apartment block. I was able to take a good look at the building. Part of my Army training was to sum up a situation. I probably saw a lot more than Raimundo did. He was driving as I wanted to examine the set-up I was going to walk into.

Along the sidewalk in front of the entrance to the apartments was a line of parked cars. As we crawled by them I spotted a Buick in which two men were sitting. There was no one hanging around the entrance to the block which was in darkness. To the left of the block was a builder's crane, its long steel arm stretching up to the top floor positioned immediately over the roof. The feet of the crane were in a vacant lot, high with weeds, and there was a big hoarding announcing another apartment block was to be built there.

'How do you see it, soldier?' Raimundo asked.

'I'll climb the crane.'

He gaped at me.

'You'll never do it. That goddam crane is twenty storeys high.'

'That's the way I'm going. It's the only way.'

'You think Savanto's men haven't thought of that?'

'Sure. So what do they do? They put a man or a couple of

men in the vacant lot to see no one gets near the crane.' I looked intently at him. 'You and I will fix them ... then up I go.'

'It's a pipe dream, soldier. You'll never get up there.'

'I'm going to bed. We do the job tomorrow night. By that time the guards will have got slack. It's tricky, but it can be done.'

When we got back to the hotel, I stripped off and took a shower. By the time Raimundo had taken his shower I was asleep.

I have this knack of relaxing before a dangerous operation. During my years in the Army I had schooled myself to sleep. I had all day tomorrow to think about what I had to face the following night: now was the time to sleep.

I came awake with a start to find Raimundo shaking me. The morning sunlight was coming through the faded blind, making me screw up my eyes.

'Wake up! Listen to this!' Raimundo was saying and the note in his voice brought me fully awake.

A voice was talking on the radio on the bedside table.

'Mr. Bill Hartley claims he saw the killing,' the voice said. 'When the police arrived with Mr. Hartley after he had raised the alarm the bodies he claimed to have seen had disappeared. There was no evidence that the shooting had occurred. The police are continuing their enquiries but Chief of Police Terrell has hinted that this could be a hoax. We have Mr. Bill Hartley with us in the studio.

'Mr. Hartley, you tell me you are a bird watcher and you often go to the Cypress swamp early in the morning to observe wild life. That is correct?'

A voice like gravel going down a chute said: 'Yeah. I don't give a damn what the police say. I saw this killing. I was up a tree with my glasses and I saw these two ...'

'Just a moment, Mr Hartley. Could you give us a description of these two people you saw?'

'Why, sure. I told the police. There was a man and a woman. The man was a giant. He looked around seven foot to me: thin, swarthy and wearing a pair of black cotton trousers. The woman was blonde and pretty and she was wearing a white bra and white slacks. The thing I particularly noticed about her was her hair was cropped short like a boy's. Well, these two were running along the sand. He was hanging on to her hand, dragging her along ...'

'Mr. Hartley, how far do you reckon you were from these two?'

'How far? Five hundred yards, perhaps a little more. I use very powerful glasses.'

'They were running along the beach. Did you get the impression that they were running away from someone?'

'I certainly did. They looked like frightened people and they were running like hell.'

'Then what happened, Mr. Hartley?'

'They got shot. There were only two shots. The first shot hit the woman. It was a head shot. She fell down and rolled into the surf. The man went down on his knees beside her and there was a second shot. He was hit in the head. I saw the spray of blood and he dropped face down on the woman. It was a hell of a thing to see.'

'What did you do, Mr. Hartley? You didn't see the killer?'

'No, I didn't see him, but from the sound of the gun he wasn't far from me. I was scared and shocked as you can imagine. The tide was coming in fast. After five or six minutes, I got down from the tree. It took me half an hour to reach a phone. I called the police. They came out pretty fast. I took them to the place where these two were shot, but by that time the tide had come in. There were no bodies, no footprints, no nothing. The police think I'm a nut, but . . .'

I turned off the radio.

Raimundo said quietly, 'I warned you, soldier . . . I'm sorry.'

I felt a trickle of cold sweat run down my face and I flicked it away with my finger.

'I had lost her anyway,' I said.

I thought of Lucy, her laugh when she was happy, the way her bottom twitched, her freckles and her eyes that scared easily. Yes, I had lost her in every sense now. She had found this long slob and she had said they thought alike. Thinking about them, I realised they would have made a better pair than she and I had done.

I lay back on the bed, staring up at the ceiling.

'Ask them to send up coffee,' I said and closed my eyes.

A bright-eyed, coloured boy came up with a tray of coffee. As he set it down, I said, 'Do you want to earn five dollars?'

His eyes grew round.

'I sure do.'

'Is there a sports' store around here?'

'A sports' store? Yeah . . . at the end of the block.'

'I want a Levison hunting knife: I want two of them. They cost around thirty dollars each. There's five bucks in it for you if you go along and get them for me.'

He gaped at me, a little uneasily.

'A Levison hunting knife?'

'That's it. They'll stock it. Okay?'

He nodded, looking from me to Raimundo and from Raimundo back to me.

'Give him the money,' I said.

Raimundo took out his two one hundred dollar bills and gave one of them to the boy.

'Well, it's your money,' the boy said. 'I'll get them if that's what you want,' and he left the room.

'What's the idea?' Raimundo asked.

I poured the coffee.

'Knives are silent,' I said.

*

We had been lying on our beds for the past two hours. Raimundo semed to sense the mood I was in. He lay flat on his back, his eyes closed. He was probably dozing. I mourned for Lucy and I buried her. It was a mental thing, but realistic. I gave her the funeral I thought she would like with lots of flowers and organ music and a tall, dignified-looking padre. I even said a prayer for her: the first prayer I've said since I was a kid. I then thought over the six months we had spent together, picking out the highlights, then I closed the memory book. It had a lock on it and I turned the key and threw the key away. There were now other things to think about. I didn't imagine I would think of her again. I had lost a lot of buddies during the war. I had gone to their funerals, but never to a memorial service. When I say goodbye, there is nothing else to say.

'When Savanto gets a hole in his head,' I said suddenly, 'what will you do?'

Raimundo lifted his head from the pillow and looked at me.

'It's a pipe dream, soldier. I wish I could make you believe it.'

'Don't answer the question if you don't want to. Why should I care?'

There was a long pause as Raimundo studied me.

'If he did get a hole in his head,' he said finally, 'I'd go back to my wife and kids in Caracas.'

'So you have a wife and kids?'

'Yeah . . . four kids . . . three boys and a girl.'

'With Timoteo dead and the old animal dead . . . what happens?'

145

'I guess Lopez will become Boss. There's no one else.'

'What sort of man is he?'

'Short of brains but peaceful.'

'Would he take care of you?'

'I wouldn't want his care. He would leave me alone. That's all I would want. I have a farm. My wife looks after it. With me working with her, it would become something important.'

'So you have something to plan for . . . a future?'

He got the message.

'I guess I have.'

There came a tap on the door.

I whipped Raimundo's automatic from under my pillow and covered it in my hand with the bed sheet.

'Open up,' I said softly. 'Get your back to the wall and swing the door open slowly.'

Raimundo was off the bed and by the door in a smooth, silent flash. Watching him, I knew he was going to be a useful man to have with me when the crunch came. He turned the key and eased open the door.

I was ready to shoot, but when I saw the coloured boy standing in the doorway, his eyes rolling, I left the gun under the sheet and brought my hand into sight.

'I've got those knives,' he said.

'Come on in,' I said and got off the bed.

A Levison hunting knife is special. It has a six-inch blade of the finest steel and is so sharp that if you draw the blade along your arm, you're shaved. It is beautifully balanced and with a finger grip handle covered with a sponge jacket. If your hand is soaking with sweat you can be sure the knife won't turn or slip. I never went into the jungle during my Army days without a Levison knife. It had saved my life a number of times. When the pressure is on, it's a man's best friend.

I checked both knives, then gave the boy a five dollar bill after he had given me the change out of the hundred dollar bill.

'I want two steak sandwiches and beer up in an hour,' I said to him. 'Steak . . . not hash.'

When he had gone, I tossed one of the knives in its leather sheath on to Raimundo's bed.

'Do you know how to use a knife?'

He gave a crooked smile.

'A lot better than you, soldier. I was born with a knife in my hand.'

I asked him the question that had been nagging at my mind ever since I knew Lucy was dead.

'What will they do with the bodies?'

'She'll go into the swamp. He will be flown back to Caracas. The old man will stage a funeral. He likes funerals.'

'Then it's just too bad he can't stage his own funeral,' I said.

We spent the day in the bedroom. We listened to the radio. The midday news said there was no further development about the two people Bill Hartley claimed he had seen shot to death. The police were checking on missing people, but so far they hadn't come up with anyone matching the descriptions of the people Hartley had said had died. The radio announcer, by the tone of his voice, seemed to be hinting that Hartley was yet another nut.

Around 22.00 we checked out of the hotel. The old negro clerk seemed relieved to see us go. He was a wise old man and he probably guessed we were cooking up something bad. I was sure the golf bag with its leather hood hadn't fooled him, but I didn't worry about him. A hotel of this rating wouldn't survive if it had trouble with the police.

Raimundo put the golf bag and the suitcase in the Volkswagen and he got under the wheel.

We had gone over the plan of operation. Raimundo still didn't think we could get away with it, but he was a little more confident.

He drove to the main shopping centre and parked near an all-night self-service store. We were far enough away from the Imperial Hotel not to worry about Savanto's button men. While he waited in the car, I went into the store. I bought a pair of heavy leather gloves. I would need them for my long climb up the steel structure of the crane. I bought a dozen sandwiches and a family-sized bottle of Coke. I bought a small rucksack in which to carry the stuff.

I joined Raimundo and we headed towards the Imperial Hotel. This was the danger zone. The button men would know I had a Volkswagen. Although there were a number of these cars driving around Paradise City, I was sure every red Volkswagen would now be scrutinized. So when we got to the beginning of Paradise Boulevard, the mile and a half long promenade by the sea where the best hotels were, I told Raimundo to park the car.

He found a hole in a row of cars and parked. We looked at each other.

'Give me ten minutes start,' I said, 'then come after me.'

There were a lot of people wandering up and down the boulevard. In that crowd we had a good chance to get lost, but Raimundo had the tricky job. He was carrying the golf bag. You don't walk along a boulevard at 22.00 carrying a bag of golf clubs. He could attract the attention of an inquisitive cop. We had discussed this. Raimundo said it would be all right. If he saw a cop he would go up to him and ask him for a cheap hotel. He would have the suitcase with him. If questioned, he would say he had hitched into town and was on vacation. That would explain the golf bag.

'Don't forget the rucksack,' I said as I got out of the car. 'I could be up there some time. I don't reckon to starve.'

'You look after your end of it, soldier. I'll look after mine.'

I paused, looking at him.

'It's going to work out,' I said.

He shrugged.

'I'm beginning to think it might.'

I set off, moving through the crowds. I moved steadily, not fast, because everyone on the promenade, under the coloured lights, was strolling and enjoying themselves. I kept a look out for anyone who might be a button man.

It took me ten minutes, weaving through the crowds, to get within sight of the Imperial Hotel. I paused, finding a space between a boy and a girl and a girl on her own who were leaning on the rails, watching the guys and dolls in the sea.

I saw lights were on in Savanto's suite. I was too far away to be able to see if he was on the balcony.

The lone girl said softly, 'Do you want some fun?'

I didn't even look at her. I moved on.

It took me another ten minutes to reach the back of the building lot. I was now away from the crowds. If I met anyone it was almost sure to be one of Savanto's men. I had the Levison knife in my hand as I slid into the darkness enveloping the building lot.

I paused for some moments, listening and looking, but there was no one around. I dropped into the long grass and the high weeds. My Army training had taught me to slide over this kind of ground like a snake. After a while I got within sight of the steel feet of the crane. I lay still, listening and watching. It took me several minutes to convince myself there was no one guarding the crane. I looked up at its great height and at the overhanging arm faintly outlined against the night sky. Savanto's men were not doing their job, but the crane must have seemed to them to be no risk. Even to me, looking up at that height, the thought of climbing that structure made me flinch. They had probably surveyed the crane and had decided no one could climb it so why waste a man, sitting in the weeds, when he could be doing something more useful?

I got to my feet and walked back to the dirt road leading to the building lot. I sat down in the shadows and waited for Raimundo. I wanted to smoke, but that would be too dangerous. So I sat and waited.

I saw him before he saw me and I called softly to him. He came out of the darkness, the golf bag on his shoulder, the rucksack on his back.

'There's no one here,' I said.

He stood beside me and looked up at the arm of the crane.

'What did you expect? No one's going up there, soldier, and that includes you.'

'Give me the rucksack,' I said.

'You're really going to try?'

'Give me the rucksack.'

I took it from him, then found the leather gloves, which I put on. I slid my arms through the straps of the rucksack and got it on my back.

Then a thought dropped into my mind. I had checked and loaded the rifle. I wasn't going to make the same mistake. I unzipped the hood of the golf bag and lifted the rifle out. It took me only a few seconds to assure myself the rifle was still loaded and ready to fire.

'I'm not blaming you, soldier,' Raimundo said as I put the rifle back.

'I'm killing this old animal,' I said. 'I'm not making any more mistakes. Go back to your wife and kids. You have a future. Enjoy it.'

We looked at each other in the faint moonlight for a long moment.

'So long, soldier,' he said. 'I hope you make the climb.'

Then he melted away into the darkness and I was on my own.

Chapter Nine

I checked my watch before I began to climb. The time was 22.40. I looked across at the distant Imperial Hotel. It was ablaze with lights. Savanto's suite, on the top floor, also showed lights.

It was a hot night. The chances were he would be on the balcony, but if he was in his bedroom or his sitting-room, I was sure I could still nail him with the telescopic sight to help me.

But luck had to fall my way. He might not be in the suite, but if he wasn't, why the lights?

I hauled myself up into the steel structure of the crane. I found it was an easy climb. It was now a matter of endurance. I told myself I had to pace myself like a runner in a marathon. The golf bag didn't help. Every so often it got caught between the cross bars and pulled me up short. I had to pause while I disentangled it. When I was level with the fifth floor of the building, I stopped to look down into the darkness.

Storm clouds were rolling across the sky. Sometime during the night it would rain. I knew the signs and welcomed them. With the clouds moving before the gentle wind, the moon was being continually obscured. I was sure anyone looking up the crane wouldn't see me.

I wedged myself between the cross bars to rest. If I rushed this climb and reached the roof exhausted and ran into one of Savanto's killers, I wouldn't stand a chance.

I sat there, relaxing, looking across at the Imperial Hotel. There were a number of people on the five balconies on Savanto's floor. From this level and from this distance I became uncertain which was his suite. Each balcony had a frosted glass partition, giving privacy. I counted from the far end and decided the third balcony suite must be Savanto's. Lights showed there, but there was no one on the balcony.

After resting for five minutes or so, I began to climb again. When I reached the tenth floor, I rested. Far below, I could see headlights as cars crawled along the traffic-congested boulevard. Away to my right I had an uninterrupted view of the beach and the sea. There were a lot of people swimming. Most of the beach was floodlit. Night bathing is one of the main attractions of Paradise City.

I went up to the fifteenth floor. I was glad I was wearing gloves. Even with gloves, my hands were getting sore. The constant gripping on the steel girders as I pulled myself up was turning into hard work. By taking it slowly, although sweating in the heat, I was still breathing easily and that was the important thing. I rested again. I saw the lights go out in two of the top suites of the hotel, but the suite I was now sure belonged to Savanto remained lit.

The next stage of the climb took me to the overhanging arm of the crane which brought me level with the penthouse and its flat roof. Black clouds now crawled across the face of the moon and blotted out the penthouse just below me.

When I reached the arm of the crane I rested again. I saw a streak of distant lightning break the darkness of the clouds. There came a faint rumble of thunder. I had lived long enough in this district to know that it wouldn't be for another hour before the storm broke.

I looked down into the darkness. Very faintly, I could make out the roof of the penthouse. I wedged the golf bag securely between two girders. My next move was to get rid of the guards if they were up on the roof. I waited for some moments, watching and listening, but I heard nothing and saw no movement on the roof just below me. Leaving the golf bag, I climbed along the arm of the crane until I reached the hanging hook. Here, I remained for some minutes. I looked across at the Imperial Hotel. The suite I was sure belonged to Savanto still showed lights, but the other suites were now in darkness. I couldn't see anyone on the balcony. Maybe, I thought, my luck was beginning to run out.

I reached forward and caught hold of the cable from which the big hook was hanging and slid down the cable on to the roof. I took off my gloves and tucked them into my belt, then my hand closed around the sponge-covered handle of my knife. I pulled the knife from its sheath.

I moved around the roof of the penthouse, surveying the terrace below. Then it slowly dawned on me that there were no guards on the terrace. Every so often the storm clouds uncovered the moon and I could see the terrace below me clearly.

Had I walked into a trap? No one guarding the crane and now, no one on the roof.

I paused to think, remembering the geography of the apartment block. It had three entrances and four elevators. None of the elevators operated after 18.00 when the agent closed down for the night. I put myself in the place of Savanto's button men. Why walk up twenty flights of stairs to guard the roof when they could seal off the building by guarding the entrances, elevators and staircases? It was slack security, but it made sense.

I slid off the roof down on to the terrace, still moving silently, still holding the knife ready for action. It took me only a few minutes to convince myself that I was alone on the terrace.

I walked to the parapet surrounding the terrace and looked across at the Imperial Hotel. I could see the lights in Savanto's sitting-room. There was no movement. No one seemed to be in the room or on the balcony.

There was time, I told myself. Now I was sure I was alone, I could fetch the Weston & Lees.

I put on my gloves and climbed back on to the penthouse roof. It was a struggle to climb the cable and get back on to the arm of the crane, but I did it. I went along the arm of the crane, collected the golf bag and made the return journey. As I began to move from cross bar to cross bar I began to wonder if it wasn't all too easy. Was it possible Savanto had already gone back to Caracas? Was this the answer why the crane wasn't guarded and there was no one on the roof? Could this be the answer?

It wouldn't be until I looked through the telescopic sight into the distant room that I could tell. Maybe I would find some wealthy tourist installed in there instead of Savanto.

I took the golf bag down on to the terrace, slid out the rifle and lay flat, resting the rifle barrel on the parapet. I clipped on the telescopic sight, screwed on the silencer, then putting the rifle butt to my shoulder, I looked through the sight. A quick turn of the focusing screw brought the room into sharp focus.

On the far wall of the room I saw the silver trout which I had noticed when I had first visited Savanto and I knew I was looking into the right room. I shifted the sight to take in the dark balcony. I picked up two lounging chairs: neither of them was occupied.

So I had to wait. Well, I had learned to wait. If luck was still running my way, Savanto would eventually come out on to the balcony. I was certain, from this range, once I had his head lined up in the cross wires of the sight, I could kill him.

Aware that the storm clouds were building up, feeling the heat of the night, I lay there, sweating, but relaxed. Every so often I looked through the sight, but I didn't keep my eye glued to it. I wanted my eye to be relaxed when I took in the slack of the trigger.

Then suddenly I saw a movement in the sitting-room: a figure crossed before one of the standard lamps. I shifted the butt of the rifle into my shoulder and my eye went to the rubber eye-cup of the sight.

In the sight, I picked up a blonde woman as she came out on to the balcony. I felt a surge of bitter disappointment run through me. So Savanto had gone! My suspicions had been right. Someone else had taken the suite.

Then I felt a creepy sensation crawl up my spine and my mouth turned dry. I was sweating badly and my body heat was so great that the eye-piece of the sight misted over.

Frantically I took out my handkerchief and wiped the eye-piece and then my face. I again looked through the sight.

The woman, standing on the balcony, the light from the sitting-room lighting her hair, looking exactly like Lucy!

I looked again. My heart skipped a beat and then began to race. It was Lucy! Lucy whom I had thought dead! Lucy whom I had mourned and buried! It was Lucy!

Then I saw a movement and I slightly shifted the sight. A tall, lean man was now standing by her side. It was Timoteo. There could be no mistake. Lucy and Timoteo were standing together on the balcony looking towards me!

'They make a handsome couple, don't they, Mr. Benson?' Savanto said quietly from out of the darkness.

I dropped the rifle and rolled over. I could just see his square-shaped figure outlined against the white wall of the penthouse. He was standing some fifteen feet away from me.

I was too shocked to move or say anything. I just lay there, supported by my elbows, staring up at him.

'I am alone and unarmed,' Savanto said. 'I wish to talk to you. Will you listen to what I have to say?'

My hand closed around the sponge-covered grip of the hunting knife. I half drew the knife from its sheath.

'I have some cigarettes,' he said. 'It is against my doctor's orders, but I find I can't resist them. Will you smoke, Mr. Benson?'

I looked across at the distant balcony. Lucy and Timoteo were no longer there. Had I imagined I had seen them? Although I had the urge to kill this man I knew I couldn't kill him with the knife. My years of training had made a rifle an impersonal weapon, but a knife to me was very personal.

I got to my feet and walked away from him. I sat on the parapet. He struck a match. He lit a cigarette and the flame of the match showed me he had aged and his black, snake's eyes no longer glittered.

'In a few hours, Mr. Benson,' he said, 'your wife and my son will be in Mexico City. From there, they will go somewhere else. I don't know where, but it is necessary for their safety to disappear. You have lost a wife and I have lost a son. I regret what has happened. I regret that you were involved. We have a saying in my country: a man can get struck by a thunderbolt. This means that a man can meet a woman and a thunderbolt hits him. When Timoteo met your wife this happened. It also happened to her. It doesn't often happen, but when it does, my people respect it, and I am forced to respect it too. Please think carefully, Mr. Benson. You are intelligent enough to know that your wife isn't the woman for you. If you can accept this truth then the loss of your wife will be less sad to you than the loss of my son is to me. They are going to be happy together. You and I will be unhappy, but this is the way of life. I came here to explain all this to you. Raimundo, who is very loyal to me, arranged this meeting. I know you want to kill me.' He lifted his heavy shoulders. 'That is understandable. I am an old man and I don't fear death. But, first let me explain. Raimundo has already explained about Diaz Savanto. I now admit I made a grave mistake. I misjudged my son and I now know he hasn't the qualifications to take my place. I must have funds if I am to improve the lot of my people. You know all about that. I couldn't foresee the thunderbolt would strike my son. When he ran away with your wife, the situation became dangerous. I love my son and I couldn't have ordered his death although the traditions of my people demand it. I am necessary to my people. The man who would take my place has no spine.' He dropped the butt of his cigarette on to the terrace and put his foot on it. 'So, something had to be arranged. When one has money and influence as I have, Mr. Benson, it is easy to make arrangements. I had to convince Lopez that my son had been executed. Since my son ran away with a woman, Lopez had also to be convinced she too had died. Hartley, the bird watcher, was easy to bribe. Money buys most things. Lopez heard Hartley's broadcast, but he wasn't entirely convinced. I reckoned on that. I have learned to be thorough. It is the only way to succeed. Lopez was shown the bodies. I have a good man who is an expert mortician. He arranged everything. Your wife and my son were heavily drugged. The mortician arranged realistic-looking head wounds which could be wiped away with a sponge. Lopez was convinced. Now they are safe to go to Mexico City and to go from there somewhere else to begin a new life. I have lost a son. You have lost a wife. I am sorry for both of us.'

I thought of Lucy. I remembered her cry: *I love him!* I had lost her anyway and the whole thing suddenly became a bore.

'I am sorry about the brand, Mr. Benson,' Savanto went on. 'I was forced to do it. There are spies everywhere who report back to Lopez what I am doing. I had to convince Lopez that I meant business if I was to save my son's life. I regret it very much.'

My hatred of him was so great that I found I was shaking.

'Okay, old man,' I said, trying to keep my voice steady. 'You have talked me out of killing you. But I am sorry for these peasants you say you are trying to help. A man like you who has such a dangerous mind can never help anyone but himself. But why should I care?' I stood up. 'So my wife and your spineless son have a happy future. That's fine. So you remain the boss of an organisation that will use vice and drugs to better the lives of a quarter of a million peasants. But I think these peasants would rather starve if they knew the filth of your money. You are just another gangster enjoying power. You are just another dirty thug hiding behind a screen of goodwill. Men like you aren't fit to live, and men like you make me want to vomit.'

I started across the terrace towards the crane.

'Mr. Benson ...'

I paused.

'I understand your anger and your bitterness,' Savanto said. 'I wish to make reparations. Take these bonds. They will compensate you for losing your wife and for the brand. Please take them.'

I saw he was holding out an envelope.

Then I realised how I could really hurt him as I wanted to hurt him.

'Okay, I'll take them,' I said.

I took the envelope from his hand. I checked to see that the envelope contained the two twenty-five thousand dollar bonds.

'Fifty thousand dollars, Mr. Benson ... it is a large sum of money,' Savanto said. 'You can now begin to make a new life.'

'Why are you giving me this money?' I asked. 'Is it a bribe to keep my mouth shut? So that when you get around to killing your nephew you will know I won't squeal to the police?'

'No, Mr. Benson. I think you deserve compensation. I regret very much what has happened.'

I moved away from him. My hand went into my trousers' pocket and I took out my cigarette lighter. I flicked it alight and held the flame to the envelope.

It gave me immense satisfaction to watch fifty thousand dollars catch fire and become smoking ash which I dropped at my feet.

I heard Savanto catch his breath. He started to his feet, making a hissing sound through his teeth.

'How could you do such a thing!' he screamed. His voice was shaking with rage. 'Goddam you! That money could have started a school for my people! It could have fed thousands of them for weeks!'

'Then why didn't you give it to them?' I said. 'You gave it to me. You gave it to me because your stinking, rotten conscience troubles you. If your peasants had the guts they would treat your money as I treat it.'

As I started towards the arm of the crane, I saw a movement out of the darkness. I stopped, my hand dropping on the handle of the knife.

'You can go down by the elevator, soldier,' Raimundo said as he moved out of the shadows. 'It's quicker and easier.'

He came into the moonlight, then he opened the french windows that led into the penthouse apartment.

I turned to Savanto.

'Screw you . . . and screw your peasants,' I said.

Then I walked through the luxuriously furnished room, lit by the moon.

Raimundo moved ahead of me and led me into the lobby and to the elevator.

He thumbed the button and the door slid open.

We looked at each other.

'That was a mistake, soldier,' he said. 'He won't forgive that.'

'I'm even with him,' I said. 'That hurt him more than a bullet.'

Raimundo looked sadly at me, then shrugged.

'Well, you did it. So long, soldier.'

I entered the elevator cage.

'Screw you too,' I said, and thumbed the button to close the doors.

I rode down the twenty floors. As I started across the lobby to the street, I saw two men sitting on the stairs, smoking: little men in dark suits, straw hats with brown flat faces and eyes like black olives. They stared at me as if they wanted to remember me again. Savanto's button men. Savanto ... the saviour of peasants!

I didn't give a damn about them.

As I walked out into the hot night, rain began to fall. Lightning lit up the sky and thunder crashed overhead. I kept walking to where I had left the car. I was quickly soaked. With rain dripping down my face, I reached the Volkswagen.

I got in, started the engine and turned on the wipers. For a long moment I stared into the darkness, thinking. I was glad I had done what I had done.

I had spat in the face of an animal.

Then I shoved the gear stick forward and headed back home: an empty home that would be lonely without Lucy, but at least a home.

Extract from: *Paradise City Herald*

STOP PRESS
Latest

Late this evening, Detective Tom Lepski, Paradise City Police, found the dead body of Jay Benson lying on the verandah of Mr. Benson's lonely bungalow at Western Bay.

Mr. Benson had been shot in the head.

'This is gang murder,' Chief of Police Frank Terrell stated. 'Benson had been branded with the symbol of the Red Dragon, a known organisation dealing in drugs and vice.'

Jay Benson, one-time top Army marksman, had recently bought the Nick Lewis School of Shooting.

The police are trying to find Mrs. Lucy Benson who is missing.

Detective Tom Lepski told our reporter: 'Benson was a nice guy. I met his wife; she was nice too.'

Crime fiction – now available in Panther Books

James Hadley Chase

One Bright Summer Morning	£1.50	☐
Tiger by the Tail	95p	☐
Mission to Venice	90p	☐
Strictly for Cash	£1.50	☐
What's Better than Money?	£1.50	☐
He Won't Need it Now	£1.50	☐
Just the Way it Is	£1.50	☐
Mission to Siena	90p	☐
You're Dead Without Money	£1.50	☐
Coffin From Hong Kong	£1.50	☐
Like a Hole in the Head	£1.50	☐
There's a Hippie on the Highway	£1.50	☐
Want to Stay Alive?	90p	☐
The Vulture is a Patient Bird	£1.50	☐
This Way for a Shroud	£1.50	☐
Just a Matter of Time	£1.50	☐
Not My Thing	£1.50	☐

Georgette Heyer

Penhallow	£1.50	☐
Duplicate Death	£1.50	☐
Envious Casca	£1.50	☐
Death in the Stocks	£1.50	☐
Behold, Here's Poison	£1.50	☐
They Found Him Dead	£1.25	☐
The Unfinished Clue	£1.75	☐
Detection Unlimited	£1.50	☐
Why Shoot a Butler?	£1.50	☐
A Blunt Instrument	£1.50	☐
No Wind of Blame	£1.50	☐

To order direct from the publisher just tick the titles you want
and fill in the order form.

All these books are available at your local bookshop or newsagent, or can be ordered direct from the publisher.,